The
Gold
Rush
Kid

BY MARY WALDORF

CLARION BOOKS
NEW YORK

For Mother

Clarion Books
an imprint of Houghton Mifflin Harcourt Publishing Company
215 Park Avenue South, New York, NY 10003

The text was set in 12-point Berkeley.

www.clarionbooks.com

Printed in the U.S.A.

Library of Congress Cataloging-in-Publication Data
Waldorf, Mary.
The gold rush kid / by Mary Waldorf.
p. cm.
Summary: When their mother dies in 1897, twelve-year-old Billy McGee and his angry, older sister leave Skagway, Alaska, to find their father, who is trekking north to the Klondike to prospect for gold.
ISBN 978-0-618-97730-7
1. Klondike River Valley (Yukon)—Gold discoveries—Juvenile fiction. [1. Klondike River Valley (Yukon)—Gold discoveries—Fiction.
2. Brothers and sisters—Fiction.] I. Title.

PZ7.W1463Go 2008
[Fic]
2007041472

MP 10 9 8 7 6 5 4 3 2 1

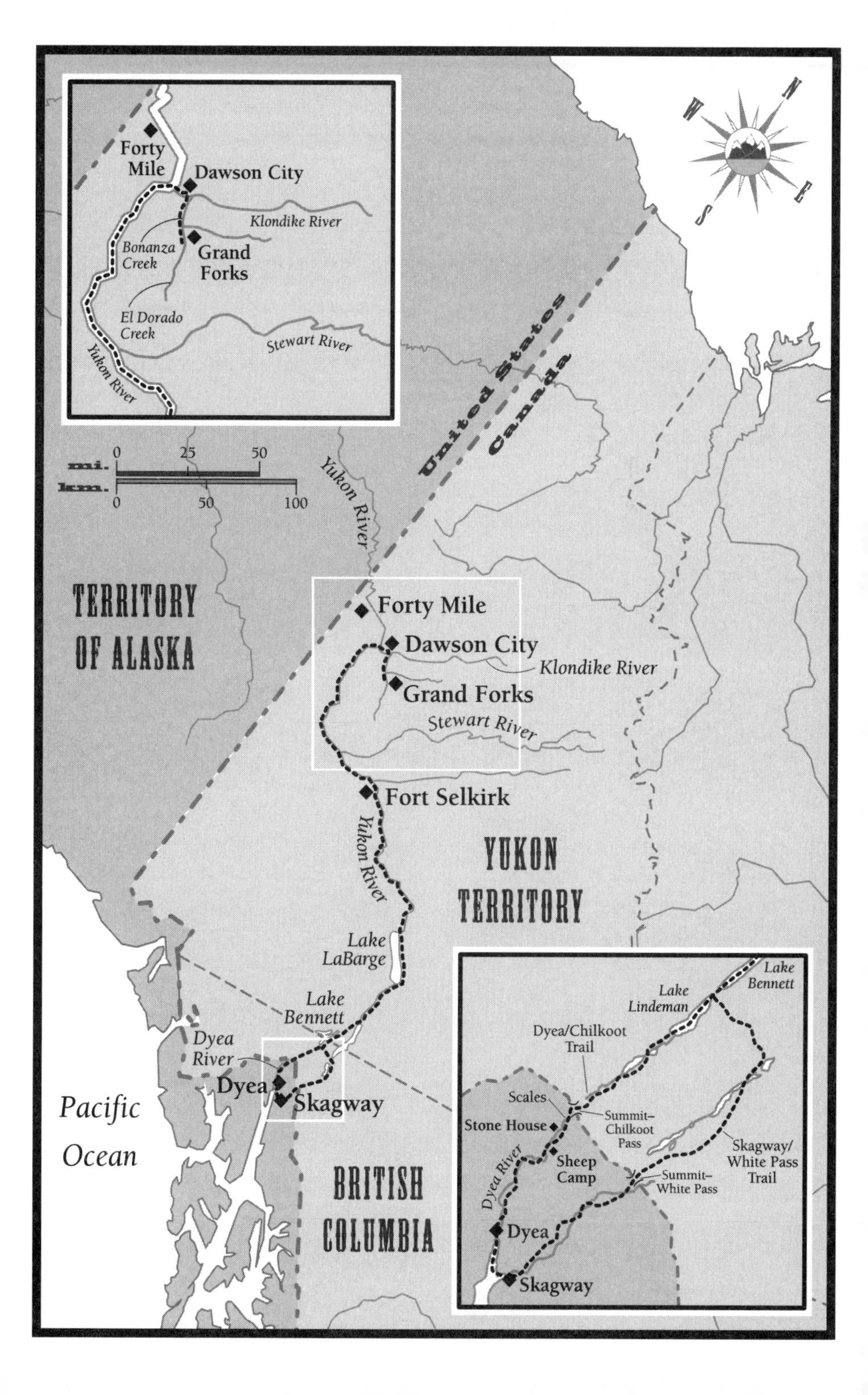

Forty Mile
Dawson City
Klondike River
Bonanza Creek
Grand Forks
El Dorado Creek
Stewart River
Yukon River
N
E
S
W
mi.
0
25
50
km.
0
50
100
United States
Canada
Yukon River
TERRITORY OF ALASKA
Forty Mile
Dawson City
Klondike River
Grand Forks
Stewart River
Fort Selkirk
Yukon River
YUKON TERRITORY
Lake LaBarge
Lake Bennett
Dyea River
Dyea
Skagway
Pacific Ocean
BRITISH COLUMBIA
Lake Bennett
Lake Lindeman
Dyea/Chilkoot Trail
Scales
Summit–Chilkoot Pass
Stone House
Sheep Camp
Dyea River
Summit–White Pass
Skagway/White Pass Trail
Dyea
Skagway

1

MY SISTER, ED

WHAT WOKE ME UP was the gritty sound scissors make when they are going through a great wad of hair. And that's what it was—my sister, Edna Rose, standing in the middle of our tent cabin, sawing off one of her thick brown braids. The other one was already lying on the dirt floor.

"Edna Rose," I said, "what in the name of good sense are you doing?"

"What's it look like?" She had her teeth set firm and spoke right through them. "And my name ain't Edna Rose no more."

It hadn't been hardly a week since the neighbors took up a collection to help us bury our mother after she took sick of typhoid and died. Edna Rose nursed Ma as best she could but had been dry-eyed at the funeral, and I thought maybe grief had caught up with her and made her a little crazy. I decided I'd check.

"What is your name, then?"

"It's Ed, like short for Edwin. Could be Edwin Ross McGee. That'd make it easier to change a piece of paper with my old name on it."

While she talked, she went on sawing at what was left of her hair. She caught my look and laid down the scissors.

"Never you mind, Billy," she said. "Ma is gone, and things have changed. I'm your big brother now, and you and me are about to set off together on the gold rush trail."

I was sure then that sorrow had unsettled her mind. "I'm feeling pretty low myself," I said, "but I guess we've got to bear up as best we can. Whacking off your hair don't seem much help, Edna Rose." That was as far as I got trying to be nice before she walloped me so hard, I near fell off the cot.

"What did you do that for?" I asked, whimpering.

"So's you'd remember my name is Ed," she said. "Now, get up and listen to me. I'm Ed McGee, like I said, and eighteen years old, although undergrown, like all us McGees, and you're the same, being sixteen and short, too."

"Nobody's gonna believe such a tale," I said. "You were only sixteen in April, and folks still call me sonny, even if I am fully twelve years."

"They will too believe it," she said, very earnest and sitting beside me. "Folks will believe almost anything if you stick close to your story and look 'em straight in the eye when you say it. I seen that happen more than once, and we can do it, too. It's our only way out of going back to Tacoma, and Aunt Lily and Uncle Peter feeling sorry for us but making us work for our keep just the same, then giving us lectures about our foolhardy pa and how he drove Ma to her death. I know they will, and you know it, too."

I drew my sleeve across my eyes and sat hunched over on the edge of the cot, thinking about Ma. When they heard about the gold strike, she and Pa figured they were going to make their fortune after years of hardly enough to eat because Pa lost his job when the lumber mills closed. He would go up to the Klondike and make a claim, and Ma and us would go as far as Skagway and wait for him there while Ma washed and mended clothes for other folks. When Pa came back with his bag of nuggets, we'd be waiting for him, as fine as you please.

Ma was still talking about how that was going to happen, even after she took sick and the doctor said there wasn't much hope. Before I had time to turn around, it was just Edna Rose and me, alone in a tent cabin. Two, three neighbor women clucked around and called us orphans. They sold some of our stuff and passed the hat for more money to buy us steamboat tickets back to Seattle and Uncle Peter, whose name they had pried out of Ma before she died.

"But what about those tickets?" I asked.

Edna Rose got up and fetched the tin box where Ma

had kept her money. Last time I had looked it was near empty, but now it was half filled with dollar bills.

"I sold one of the tickets back," she said, "and the other one I traded for an outfit. Looky here, Billy." She dragged off a canvas tarp that Ma had used to cover the firewood, and underneath was a great pile of stuff: blankets, buckets, pots and kettles, a shovel and pickax, a pan for panning gold, and sacks of grub—flour and beans and the like.

"I met a fellow down at the beach yesterday who had taken a look at the mountains and listened to the tales of a couple of sourdoughs and decided he didn't want to strike it rich in the Yukon after all. So I traded one ticket for his outfit. Should do for the two of us until we meet up with Pa."

"And how we gonna do that, Edn—Ed?"

"We'll catch up with him, easy. You and me could always outwalk him, you know. He's big, but his legs is short, and he had a giant pack."

"Yeah," I said slowly. "Seemed like he had a lot more food than this here."

"That don't matter," she said, "'cause we'll meet up with him long afore we run through this grub."

"How do you know that? We don't even know where him and the other men are at, Edna—" I ducked because she was headed toward me, fist raised.

Just then we heard footsteps coming along the path to our place. "Quick," she hissed, "pull that tarp over the outfit." Then she went to rummaging in a satchel of

Ma's stuff, flinging stockings and drawers all about, until she found a scarf to cover her head. Just in time, too, as Missus Kettleson, our neighbor from across the way, peered through the door flap and called, "You young'uns up and about yet? I got some blueberry biscuits for your breakfast."

Missus Kettleson was a hearty woman who had come up to Skagway with her hound dog, Rusty, and a cast-iron stove. She was aiming to start a bakery and get rich off hungry prospectors. Also, she was the ring-leader in getting us fixed up with steamship tickets, so's we could go back home and be safe.

Now she stood in the doorway, dressed in boots and with a leather jacket over her calico dress, and—what interested me most—holding a plate of biscuits you could tell were still warm from the oven. Edna Rose was busy kicking hunks of hair under her cot. She had the scarf tied around her head, but anybody who looked close could see there weren't no thick hair coming out below. That is, if Edna Rose turned around, which she didn't do. Instead, she sat on the edge of the cot, hands in her lap, and said, "Ain't that nice of you. We've had our breakfast, but we'll save 'em for later. Billy, take a couple biscuits and give Missus Kettleson her plate."

Well, now, that was just the beginning of the lies that rolled off Edna Rose's tongue that day. She sat there prim as anything and told Missus K. we was nearly packed for the steamship and would most likely spend the night aboard. There wasn't a thing more she could do for us; she had done more than enough already.

But Missus K. was not so easy put off. She sat down on one of the stumps we used for chairs and said it had eased her mind considerable to know we were going back to relations—and surely we could make room for a plate of fresh biscuits?

"You bet." I grabbed the whole lot before Edna Rose could object.

"We do thank you, ma'am," Edna Rose said. "There's only one thing that worries me, and that's how will Pa know what happened?"

Missus K. had taken care of that, too. She had given the message to a party of gold hunters on horseback headed for the White Pass Trail the day before.

"But Pa and his partners went over to Dyea to take the Chilkoot Pass," Edna Rose said.

"Honey, that don't make no difference. They all have to meet up around Lake Bennett, where they build the boats. And bad news always travels fast." Missus K. spread out on our biggest stump, comfortable as if she expected to stay all day and watch us eat the biscuits, which were mighty delicious, I can tell you. I didn't know it then, but those would be the last true baked goods I was to have for some time.

"I only knew your ma for a short while," she said, sighing, "but it was enough to know she was a good person. It broke her heart to leave you two."

"We know that," Edna Rose said, real sharp. "Still,

she'd want us to get on with things, Missus Kettleson. So if you'll excuse us, we need to finish packing."

Missus K. wanted to help and to suggest where we might sell anything we had left over, but finally Rusty poked his nose in the door and whined for his grub. She hauled herself up and took her plate and dog back to the little cabin that she was fixing to turn into a bakery.

Edna Rose watched her go. "Old busybody," she said, tearing off the scarf to have another go at what was left of her hair. Ma always said that nobody in our family was going to get elected on the basis of good looks, and that meant Edna Rose, too, I supposed. She was kind of square built and had a habit of hunching her shoulders and drawing down her eyebrows as if she was getting ready to whack you. But her hair had been something wonderful, thick and brown like the burnt-sugar icing Ma put on applesauce cakes. It gave me a sorry feeling to see it lying in the dirt, and I wondered what Ma might think.

"Never mind," she said when she saw the look on my face. "I told that busybody the truth. Ma would want us to keep going. Now, sort through your stuff again. We can't take but what's absolutely necessary."

I didn't think I could let go of my treasures—books and a bag of marbles and the tin soldiers I'd had since I was a little fellow.

"No, Billy, nothing of that sort. Whatever we take we got to carry on our backs."

"But Ma give me them books, and the soldiers, too."

She turned on me fiercely. "Ma is gone and left us here on our own. You'd better get used to that."

Tears came into my eyes, but I wouldn't let go of my box of stuff.

"Oh, all right. Don't blubber," she said finally. "You can take one book. We'll bury the rest along with some of Ma's things in the tin money box. We can come back for 'em after we strike it rich."

Edna Rose laid out a few things that Ma had treasured.

"Seems like you might want to keep some of this to remember her by. How about this locket?" I held it out to her. It used to have a picture of somebody inside, I forget who, but now it was empty.

Edna Rose fingered it in silence. "All right," she said again. "Not that I need a trinket to remind me of my own ma. Now, hustle and pick out a book you want."

"Oh, Edna Rose," I said, "you're a peach."

Then she did whack me for not remembering her new name.

2

WE START OFF

THAT DAY everything came off pretty much the way Edna Rose had planned. After we had gathered all that we were going to take, leaving not much more than the stumps and packing-box table for whoever else came along, we buried the tin box amongst the huckleberry bushes and marked the place with stones.

"Hey, Ed, don't this look pretty natural? No one would think to dig here, would they?"

My sister was busy fixing up our packs. "Not a chance, Billy," she said without even turning around. "Now, run and tell Missus K. that the captain of the *Alaskan Queen* says we can sleep aboard tonight. No need for her to bother about us anymore."

As I was crossing the road—it wasn't much more than wagon ruts going north—after leaving Missus K.'s, a party of gold hunters on horseback came riding by three abreast, looking like they was going to a picnic, all smug because they didn't have to carry their outfits. There had been a regular stream of folks going by our tent cabin every day, headed for the White Pass Trail out of Skagway. We heard terrible stories about that trail, how there were boulders as big as houses, and rockslides, and drop-offs where horses were more 'n likely to fall and break their legs. But these folks didn't know that yet.

I raised my hand in a sort of salute as they went by with their gold pans and shovels bouncing alongside their packs. One of them, a woman squeezed into a fancy purple dress, waved at me. "Hello, sonny, what's your name?" she sung out. When I told her, she said, "Well, Cap'n Billy, wish us luck, and we'll bring you back some gold dust!"

I watched them trot out of sight and then hustled back to help Edna Rose stash our outfit a little ways off, where we could pick it up later. We took our grips and the carpetbag and went down the road toward the canal, saying goodbye to folks as we passed their tents and cabins.

Edna Rose had picked out a shed near the wharf where we could hide until it was dark enough to sneak back. It was the tail end of summer, and daylight lasted a long while that far north. When Edna Rose finally thought it was safe, we creeped behind the rows of rickety buildings—the trading posts, gaming houses, and saloons filled with gold hunters and people making money off them.

Just as we were coming close to our place, I heard Rusty barking. Missus Kettleson opened the door of her cabin and let him out. She stood there in the square of light a moment, then closed the door. First thing Rusty did was trot across the road to the back of our place, where Edna Rose and me was sneaking along behind the bushes.

A lucky thing I had spent time with that dog and he liked me pretty good or he would have set up a howl at finding us there. As it was, he yipped a bit and wagged his tail before he went on his belly and crawled inside the thicket and licked my face.

"Get him out of here!" Edna Rose hissed.

I patted him a couple times and then whispered, "Go get 'em, Rusty." He looked at me, puzzled, but after a moment he wriggled out and trotted off looking for something to get.

Soon we could hear Missus K. calling him, and then the square of lamplight from her doorway disappeared again. Both me and Edna Rose breathed a sigh of relief and went back to creeping until we came to the place where our stuff was hid.

She checked over the grips and the two big canvas bags we was somehow going to strap on our backs. Then she gave a low whistle.

"Tarnation, Billy, I must've left the ax and bucket in the cabin. You'll have to go fetch 'em."

I argued that what she forgot, she should get. But my sister had taken it on herself to be boss of this project, so I gave up jawing and crept back to the tent cabin. I had just got around the corner and was reaching up to push back the flap and crawl in when there was a fierce hand on my shoulder, and a second later I was lifted right up into the air.

It was Missus K. She had a shotgun under one arm, too, ready for action.

"Hey!" I said. "Leggo, Missus Kettleson. It's me, Billy."

"Was that you sneaking along the side of the road a while back?" she asked, giving me a good shake before she let me down.

"Yes, ma'am, it might've been." I was thinking fast. "Edna Rose has misplaced something and sent me back to see did she leave it here."

Of course, Missus K. wanted to know what it was, and still racing along in my thoughts, I said it was a trinket that had belonged to our ma. In that case, Missus K. said, she would fetch a lantern and help me look.

I barely had time to duck inside and grab the ax and canvas bucket and race back to where Edna Rose was figuring what clothes to wear. When I gasped out my story, she jerked off the locket she was wearing under her plaid shirt. "Good thinking, Billy. Take this and hide it quick before she gets back."

Our luck held. I had just got into the tent cabin when there came Missus K. with her lantern held high and Rusty barking happily beside her.

Me and her commenced to crawling around the dirt

floor, upturning stumps and the packing-box table, searching for a thing I had in my pocket the whole time. I let a few minutes pass before I called out, "Bring the lantern. I think I see something shining in this corner here."

Missus K. was so pleased—"Gratified" was how she put it—at finding our dear ma's locket that she took me to her place for a cup of hot cocoa, made with a powder she'd brought up from Frisco and mighty tasty, too. Then she insisted on walking with me nearly all the way back to the wharf.

I had to wait an age to make sure she had got home with Rusty and was most likely asleep before I walked clear around west of town and came into our spot from the back. I was tired by that time, but Edna Rose was chomping at the bit, ready to take to the trail. She had dressed herself in the fellow's clothes, padded underneath with strips of cloth to make them fit and with the trouser legs rolled up. She was a sight, more square than ever with all that padding and one of Pa's old hats jammed on her head with the brim turned down. She had got most of the outfit into the two canvas sacks, and the rest we stuffed into the grips and Ma's old carpetbag. That left a kettle and some pans that we had to carry to keep them from rattling until we got out of earshot. After she tied the bundle on my shoulders and handed me two grips and the kettle, I felt like I couldn't go more than a short ways. When I began to whine, she cut me short.

"This is the way it'll be from now on. So hustle, Billy. We've lost half the night already."

We set off north following close to the Skagway River. Folks called it a braided river because it split and twisted back and forth across the valley like the thick strands in Edna Rose's braids that used to be. At the north edge of town, I turned off on a path leading eastward.

"Where you going?" Edna Rose hissed at me, but she knew perfectly well, and after a bit I heard her clanking along behind.

We came to the slope where Skagway's burying ground had been laid out and to the corner where our ma was buried. A rocky mound was all there was—no sign to give her name or say when she died, let alone a stone marker. We stood for a while, looking at it in the moonlight.

"Who will know this is the grave of Rose Ellen McGee, after we're gone away?" I asked my sister.

"When we strike it rich, we'll have a stone put up."

"With her full name and where she was born in Oklahoma Territory?"

"Sure, Billy. We'll put everything on it you want. Now, let's get a move on. It's a long way to Smuggler's Cove."

The thought of a stone for Ma cheered me, and I walked along pretty well for some time, thinking about what I would get carved on it—a rose, maybe, to go with her name, and "Gone but not forgotten," like I saw in a book once. Ma and me both liked book stories, almost as much as the ones you tell out loud.

"Don't you miss that, Ed?" I said. "Ma reading with us at night?"

Edna Rose just stalked along with the tin pans bouncing against her pack and didn't bother to answer, but saved her breath for the hike over the first ridge and then the second. By that time, I was panting and groaning from the weight of the pack.

Edna Rose scoffed. "This ain't nothing," she said. "You'd do better to just keep marching instead of wasting your breath rattling on about something or other."

We hiked along the ridge until we found the trail that went down toward Smuggler's Cove, which lay between Skagway and the Dyea inlet. You might think going down would be easier than going up, but you'd be wrong. It was different, but it wasn't no easier.

It was beginning to get light. The pack thumped against my back at every step, and the grips in my hands swung forward as though to make me fall on my face. When I stumbled, Edna Rose would turn and give me a hard look before going on. Her pack was so big, her head was all I could see of her—that and two legs coming down below, trudging on and on. By the time we reached the near edge of the cove, the sun was well up.

"Now, here's my plan," Edna Rose said, as she helped me off with my pack. "We'll look for a fisherman to take us over to Dyea in his skiff. When we find one, I'll let you do the talking. Only be sure to call me Ed. If you don't, I'll make you sorry."

"Okay, okay, but couldn't we rest a little first?"

Ed agreed, only the way she said it, you'd think she didn't need a rest herself. We ducked out of sight behind some boulders and she parceled out some of Missus K.'s biscuits. Then we both fell asleep.

The sun was high in the sky when I woke to the sound of a boat hull scraping against the rocky shore. An old fellow with nearly white hair was hauling his skiff up on the beach.

"Who is it?" Edna Rose hissed.

"Well," I said, "he's probably a smuggler, this being Smuggler's Cove." She did not appreciate that and gave me a hard shove.

"Go ask him for a ride over to Dyea. Say we can pay as high as three dollars."

At first, the old fellow didn't answer, but just kept right on making things tidy in his boat. Then he shook his head. "Sonny, I been out on this bay half the morning and I'm not likely to go out again for three dollars."

Well, now, that surprised me, but I trotted back with the information. Edna Rose's face reddened. "Offer him five dollars, then," she said, and I knew that the trip over from Skagway hadn't been as easy for her as she let on.

The old man wouldn't budge for five, nor for six, neither. Said it wasn't worth it to go out again. Edna Rose had come out from behind the rocks, but still kept her distance. "Well, then," she said in a gravelly voice, "I reckon us boys'll have to hoof it to Dyea."

"I suppose you can do that, young fella, if you've got plenty of time. There's not much of a trail between here and there. Most folks go to Dyea direct or hire a boat in Skagway. How come you two hiked this far?"

I could see that made Edna Rose nervous, like she thought he might know we was going against the rules, so I put in hurriedly, "Isn't there something you'll take in trade for a ride, mister?"

"What ya got, sonny?"

"We have our outfit here. Might be something we could give up."

Edna Rose began to shift around, even more nervous at the notion of letting that old man look through our packs and big old grips, but she needn't have worried because it was pretty clear he didn't think he'd see anything of interest.

"You boys wouldn't have some reading material, would you? A magazine with stories? Now and again, I get a hankering for something fresh to read."

"Oh," I said, very casual, "we might." I turned my back so as not to see my sister's face as I dug into one of the grips and came out with the three books I'd hidden there.

I laid them out on the top of a rock. "This first one is pirates mostly, and this one is a story about a boy in England, and this one is old-time stories—you know, Greek tales and the like." I turned again to sneak a glance at Edna Rose. She looked fit to bust, 'specially when she caught sight of the size of that second book, so I added, "My ma gave these to me."

He said he was sorry to take something my mother had given me, but he had his lip set for reading and the old tales looked good.

"All right," I said. "I know most of those by heart anyhow."

All this while, Edna Rose was standing back, with her head half lowered like she was ready to run one of us down for cheating, but there wasn't much she could do except follow along as the old man—his name was Tom Thunder, he said—helped us carry our outfit down to his skiff. He was a strong oarsman, and pretty soon we was sitting easy, watching the wooded ridge above the shore slip away.

It was long after sunset when we came into Dyea inlet. In the twilight gloom, the town looked even more ramshackle than Skagway. Shacks and tents were scattered among scrubby trees at the head of a wide and shallow bay. There wasn't no wharves that we could see, and, it turned out, none that we couldn't see. Gold hunters coming in by ship had to pack their goods on rafts or lighters, if there was any around. The big boats had to anchor a ways out, Old Tom told us, and some people just threw things overboard, planning for the tide to carry them in. Horses and mules were pushed into the water and had to swim for shore. People yelled furiously, as if they was in a temper fit, throwing their stuff into the water all around every which way. Lanterns were already flickering on the bows of little boats, and bigger lanterns glowed from the masts of three ships anchored some distance from the shore.

Old Tom rowed us all the way to where his boat scraped the sand and then helped us unload and carry our stuff up the beach to a dry place. It was pretty tough going. You didn't know if you was bumping into a pile of goods or a person already bivouacked for the night. When you heard cursing, or someone whacked your leg, then you knew. Old Tom had a lantern, and I kept pretty close to him. We found a clear place finally and foraged for scraps of wood to build a little campfire. Tom made tea in one of our pots, and we all shared the rest of the biscuits and some cold bacon.

After he drained his cup, he said he was going to sleep in the boat and would set out for Smuggler's Cove at first light.

"This place is too durned crowded for me. Folks packed cheek by jowl, suckers and thieves, no way to tell which is which. You boys take my advice and turn around and go straight back."

"We're bound to find our pa," I said.

"Well, good luck to you." He nodded and off he went, with his lantern bobbing along, down to the shore.

3

DYEA BEACH

NEXT MORNING when I poked my head out of my bedroll to take a look around, I could hardly believe my eyes. Edna Rose and me were lying in the middle of the biggest camping out since the world began. Nearly the whole wide beach at Dyea was covered with tents and outfits and people. Some folks were still in their bedrolls, while others crouched by breakfast fires. All around them was piles and piles of goods—some laid up neat, but most just dumped higgledy-piggledy—boxes and barrels, canvas sacks, stoves, wheelbarrows, bedsteads, wagons, sleds, and carts. Our pile looked somewhat puny compared to the others. It had been a terrible load coming over the ridge, but here, laid out on the sand, it didn't seem such a much.

Edna Rose peered out from her blankets and got her hat fixed good on her head before she stood up.

"Get some more wood, Billy. We'll have ourselves a hot breakfast before we pack up."

The beach and way beyond it had been nearly stripped of driftwood and dead branches, so I had to go quite a distance, working my way amongst tents and outfits, before I found enough scraps for a decent fire. Folks hardly seemed to notice me or each other or anything other than their work of sorting and packing and hefting loads to see how much they could carry. Some were dressed in brand-new clothes, mackinaw jackets and wool trousers and colored suspenders, while others looked as if they had just got up out of a flophouse and come straight to Dyea for a better chance in life, like our pa was looking for. There was a few women, most of them wearing big-brimmed felt hats and long skirts already mud-streaked above their boots. There was even some children who looked as if they had been hauled out of bed too early. But mostly it was men hustling around, intent on their work.

When I got back, a young fellow with a blue enamel coffeepot in one hand was standing by our last night's fire, addressing some remark to Edna Rose.

"Hullo," I said, dropping my load of sticks.

He turned toward me with a grin. "Hullo yourself." He was hatless and had light hair that stuck out all over his head. A sort of pinkish yellow it was, and he had the white lashed eyes and eyebrows that go with it.

"I come over to offer you boys some hot coffee since it looks to be a while before your fire gets going.

But I can't get much comment out of your partner here."

That was true. Edna Rose had her chin tucked into her chest and she was studying the ground as though she thought fire might spring up if she stared hard enough. She growled something in her Ed voice that meant no.

"Then how about you, sonny?" the young fellow asked, and when I nodded, he poured me a cup of hot black coffee and one for himself and then produced a can of evaporated milk from his back pocket. He hunched down beside me while we watched Edna Rose lay the fire.

He said his name was Jack Purdy. He'd come up to Seattle from Frisco and then on to Dyea with another fellow. They was headed for the gold fields, just like everyone else, but his partner was having second thoughts.

Jack shifted on his haunches and looked around at our grips and canvas sacks. "Where's the rest of your outfit, boys?"

"That's it," I said, "and it's plenty to carry. We hauled it on foot all the way from . . ." Edna Rose gave me one of her glowering looks, and I let the rest of the sentence die off.

"Who told you this is enough gear to carry you into the Yukon?"

"The fellow we got it off was headed there, and this was his outfit."

"Maybe half his outfit," Jack said. "This don't look like enough gear and grub for one prospector, let alone two."

Edna Rose growled, "It'll do."

"Well, from what I hear, the Canadian Mounties check everyone that goes over Chilkoot Pass, to make sure they have enough grub to last through the winter, on account they don't want a lot of starving stampeders drifting around their territory. I doubt they'll let you boys through."

Edna Rose slammed down the fry pan she was getting ready for pancakes and then picked it up and whacked it down again, but she didn't speak.

I thought fast and said, "We're going to meet our pa. He already took most of our stuff."

"Oh," Jack said. "He had packers, did he?"

"Sure," I agreed, "probably him and his partners hired packers. When we get to Lake Bennett, there'll be plenty of stuff."

"That's all right, then," he said. "But if you're lacking for anything now, some folks here are selling goods at ten cents on the dollar."

"How come?"

"That's a good question," he said. "Some of 'em had a look at that pass yonder, where they'll have to manhandle every pound of gear up and over, and they got a change of heart, like my partner did. You boys might want to look over his stuff and fill in where you're short."

"Sure," I said, thinking that was a good idea, until Edna Rose broke in, her voice fierce and mean.

"Thank you for your advice, mister. Me and Bill are fine the way we are."

Jack shrugged. "If you change your mind, I'm over yonder where you see the cookstove. That's for sale, too." Then he took his coffeepot and went away.

Well, sir, Edna Rose was mad enough to fry ice, as Ma used to say. She grabbed the brand-new canvas bucket, threw it down, then stomped on it.

"That dratted slicker in Skagway cheated me for certain, passing this piddling stuff off as a real outfit. He must've thought I was a regular cheechako."

That was what the Indians called greenhorns that come into this country without knowing a thing about it.

"Seems like we are cheechakos, Edn—pardon me—Ed. Now, hold on," I rushed on, because she had already grabbed the bucket again and was about to let it fly in my direction. "Couldn't we use some of our boat-ticket money for buying grub? It should be real cheap if what the fella says is true. We could buy his partner's stuff, come to that."

"Not on your life. I don't want nothing further to do with him, after he comes pushing in here without an invite. He's nosy, one thing. You can tell that by the way his eyes slant, kind of shifty. And another thing, he thinks he knows more 'n anybody else. We'll buy from other folks, Billy."

So we spent the rest of that day checking over our stuff and then looking to see what others had that we didn't, which turned out to be mostly food. Edna Rose whispered to me what to offer, and I did all the jawing. By the end of the day, we had bags of dried onions, potatoes, more bacon, beans, flour, some dried apples, and tins of milk. When we got it all together with our Skagway outfit, there was quite a pile.

Next morning we started at dawn stuffing things into canvas sacks. But no matter how we arranged them, we couldn't get as much as a quarter of the new outfit loaded on our backs.

One time, Edna Rose got me all loaded with gear, leaving out the food altogether. Then she hung a new coffeepot on the pack, and that little weight knocked me off my balance so I fell over and lay rocking on the lumpy pack like a turtle turned on its back.

"This ain't gonna work, Ed," I said.

"Sure it is. Get up and try again." She was trying to haul me up when Jack Purdy came by, looking for a buyer for his partner's cookstove. He smiled in a kind of crooked way, then brushed my sister aside, took hold of my arms, and pulled until I came upright, swaying and looking to go down the other way. He started loosening straps.

"Hey," Edna Rose said. "Take your hands off our stuff, mister."

Jack went right on removing bundles. "If you

boys'll hold your horses, I'll tell you how folks manage. They shift their outfits part at a time, carrying one load up to the first stopping place and going back for another. When they get everything up to the first cache—that's what they call a place where you store your goods on the trail—they head off for the next stopping place."

"But, Jack, how long's that gonna take?"

The funny smile twitched at his mouth again. "It'll take you boys about as long as it takes everyone else, and that's at least two weeks to get all your goods to the top of the pass."

I felt like bawling. Pa would be so far ahead of us, we couldn't hardly hope to catch up with him.

"Of course, you boys still don't have much of an outfit," Jack said in a kindly way. "You might go a bit faster. And you don't need to worry about folks stealing your goods when they're cached. On the gold rush trail, they say that's a worse crime than murder, and justice is quick. Of course, that's not to say some folks won't try to swindle you out of something, but they usually do that to your face. So then, I guess you're not in the market for a cookstove?"

Ed snorted so fiercely, Jack chuckled and went away. Her and me just stared at each other. Finally, she took off her hat and ran her hands back and forth over her spiky hair. "Blast it all," she said. "First we get cheated by that liar in Skagway and now here's another one. Probably he aims to slow everybody else so he can get to the gold first. If he hadn't stuck his nose in our business, telling us we needed more stuff, we'd be halfway to Chilkoot Pass by now."

That argument wouldn't hold water and she knew it, but she went on ranting until she worked her way through every complaint she had stored up. Then she started packing again. "And another thing. You think I'm gonna let you carry books up there instead of grub, you better think again."

That wasn't fair, neither, since one of my books had saved us miles of walking from Smuggler's Cove. So I let the books lay at the bottom of a grip and went on hefting stuff to see how much I could put on my back and still walk.

While I worked, grim thoughts crept into my mind and I couldn't seem to hold 'em off. Suppose we never caught up with Pa? Our ticket money was gone, so we couldn't go back to Uncle Peter.

"What if we miss Pa, Ed? Suppose him and them other men has already built a boat and gone on to Dawson? What'll we do then?"

Edna Rose swung on me, eyes flashing. "You just hush with that, Billy McGee. You're always thinking on the dark side. Pa'll be there, all right. All you got to worry about now is getting this stuff up the trail."

It was midmorning before we had settled on packs we could carry. Edna Rose had been tore up about what stuff to take. Should it be what cost the most? But then we'd have to leave those very same things at the side of the trail while we came back for more. Back and forth she went, pulling out one thing and putting in another.

Finally, she settled on a first load, and we stashed the rest under some bushes with a tarp laid over and fastened down with tent stakes, the way we seen other folks do. Then me and my sister left the long, sandy beach of Dyea and headed north for the Chilkoot Pass.

It took us three days to get all our stuff up to a cache near Finnegan's Point. Most of that time Edna Rose wouldn't hardly speak to me, let alone say howdy to folks on the trail. But after we had carried everything to the first stop, she loosened up a little and fried bacon and potatoes for supper.

"You know, Billy," she said, while we were sitting around the fire afterward, "we have just as good a chance as anybody to strike it rich up there in the Yukon, you and me and Pa. As good a chance as any other of these cheechakos, don't you think?"

"Sure," I said doubtfully.

"What'll be the first thing you do when we come back with our pockets full of gold nuggets?"

"Buy a headstone for Ma's grave, so folks will know who that is lying there."

Edna Rose poked at the fire a bit. "Sure," she said, after a while. "But then what?"

"I dunno."

For some reason that sent her into a rant. "That shows that you are weak-minded, Billy. You're always thinking about what's over and done. You talk that way around Pa, and you'll bring him down."

"Likely he'll be pretty low anyway, if he's heard about Ma."

Edna Rose jumped up and went for her bedroll, to spread it out beside the fire. "Might be he'll set his face to the future, like me, and not mope over what can't be changed," she said, slapping the blankets down like they'd done her injury.

I sat for a while longer, feeling sorry for myself and wondering at Edna Rose's hard heart. It came to me that she couldn't have loved our ma so very much and might even be glad of this chance to be boss and go out on her own. I worked it up pretty good and was close to sniffling, when the thought of her hearing me dried my tears. I believe it was then that I truly got to thinking of her as Ed, instead of Edna Rose. She was still my sister, but not somebody you'd look to for any comfort. I laid my bedroll on the other side of the fire and got in, but stayed awake for a while, listening to the folks still traveling, the ones who couldn't stop, even at night, for fear somebody would get ahead of them and claim all the gold. People like my sister, Ed, keeping their faces to the fore, not weak-minded like me.

4

THE CANYON

UP TO FINNEGAN'S POINT the traveling had been fairly easy, through meadows where the alders and willows grew, and the river they called the Dyea wandered back and forth. But after Finnegan's Point the trail went into a steep-sided canyon that was gloomy even in the middle of the day. Heaps of fallen trees and roots and boulders made the going considerable slower, and worse when you had to crisscross the Dyea River, still running pretty good even so late in the year. Some places there was a rough log bridge. In others there was only slippery rocks and the cold mountain water looking mean as it swirled around them. Back home on the farm, me and Edna Rose had walked on top of rail fences and picked our way over rafters in the barn. But that was different from wobbling from one wet rock to another or keeping your balance on a slick log with fifty pounds of flour strapped to your back.

Well, we went along pretty good for a couple days, ferrying our stuff to the next stop. On the morning we were on the way back to get our last load, we crossed one of those log bridges. I remarked how much worse it had gotten from all them boots tromping on it. At the end of the bridge, the trail went along a ledge above the river. Somehow I was in the lead, and so I was the first to see Jack Purdy coming the other way. He was so heavy-loaded and bent over that I might not've recognized him, except he stopped right in front of me and backed himself and his pack against a boulder so he could rest and mop his face with a bandanna.

"Hullo, Jack," I sung out.

"Keep moving," Ed said, giving me a poke.

"Hullo, boys," Jack said. "How you doing?"

"Fine," Ed growled, and made as if to push past him, but Jack asked could we wet his bandanna in the river so he could tie it around his head and keep cooler.

"Sure," I said, and obliged while Ed stood off, scowling under her hat brim. Jack eased his big pack further against the rock and wiggled it around a little, making the cook pots clang. He said he'd lost considerable time getting rid of his partner's outfit and trying to find a new partner afterward.

"Any luck?" I asked.

"Not anybody I took a liking to. But there might be a better chance at Lake Bennett, since I can advertise myself as a boat pilot."

"Maybe Pa and his partners will be looking for a pilot."

"Billy, we need to keep moving," Ed said, and she started down the trail without so much as saying so long to Jack.

He waved his bandanna at me and then hauled himself upright from his resting spot and moved back onto the trail. His pack shifted around like it wasn't settled good, but he kept going. I took my time following Ed, thinking about how mean she had become. She'd always had a mean streak and liked to boss, but back home Ma had kept things fair. Now it looked like there was no stopping her.

I was poking along behind, still worrying over that, when I came to another rock ledge that ran alongside the river. Something caught my eye, a piece of red cloth twirling through the water. I stared at it for a moment before I knew what it was—Jack's bandanna that he maybe had dropped. I wondered if I should try to get it for him. It seemed I stood there for a while puzzling, but it must've been only a few seconds before a horrible thought jumped into my mind. I pictured that log bridge and his heavy load going off balance. I turned around and trotted back up the trail.

Ed must've looked back because I heard her yell, "Where do you think you're going?"

I didn't answer, only trotted faster, hoping I wouldn't see nothing at the bridge except the Dyea River tumbling along over the rocks, that I wouldn't see a pack with pots hung off to one side and the shape of a person lying face-down beneath it. But that is what I saw.

"Help!" I screeched. "It's Jack fell in!" I tumbled down the bank and plunged into the river up to my knees. I got hold of him all right, but couldn't budge him, with that pack pinning him down. I began to blubber, "Jack, get up now. Please, get up."

There was a spill of gravel as Ed came sliding down the bank behind me. She already had her knife out, ready to cut the straps of Jack's pack. "Come on, help me get it off him," she said.

We both tugged, and she sawed at the straps. Finally, we pulled the pack loose and dragged Jack out of the river to a level place on the shore. His eyes was closed and his face was a dusky blue. Ed punched him good and hard in the belly. Water rushed out of his mouth, but he didn't stir. She gave him another punch, which brought more water, but no other sign.

"He's gone, Billy," she said, sitting back on her haunches.

"No," I said, "no, *no*. There must be something we can do."

"I don't think so," she said, getting to her feet.

That was exactly the way the neighbor women had acted when Ma lay sick in her cot and couldn't speak. I begged them to help, but they said there wasn't a thing a body could do, and pretty soon Ma just died.

"Let's not give up. Please," I said.

Ed was wading back into the river to fetch Jack's

pack, which had lodged against some rocks further on, and I followed her, grabbing at her arm.

"Didn't you tell me about the time the hired man fell in the horse pond and Uncle Peter saved him?"

She shrugged me off at first and kept grappling with the pack, then suddenly stopped and straightened up. "That he did, Billy." The pack slid back into the water, and she reached for it again. "But that fellow had only been in the horse pond a few minutes."

"Probably Jack, too, only a few minutes. Oh, come on, Ed, please, give it a try. Please."

She considered for a moment and then let the pack go. "All right, but don't count on it."

We waded back to shore and turned Jack over with his face to one side. Ed got astride his back and splayed her hands over his rib cage, pressing real hard. She rocked back and then forward again, pressing as hard as she could.

"Keep his face to the side, Billy, and pry open his mouth so he don't choke. Tell me if you see any change."

She kept rocking forward, pressing against his ribs and falling back, over and over, but Jack's face stayed the same dusky blue and still. After a while I took her place while she crouched by his head to watch.

"I don't think it's any use, Billy," she said after a long spell of us taking turns, but the words were hardly out before she gasped, "Wait now. Keep going!" Something had passed over Jack's face. A flutter, she said. I thought

I saw it, too, and kept on rocking and pressing fiercer than before, with Ed saying, "That's right, Billy, keep going, and you, mister, you breathe. You hear me? Breathe." Just when I thought I was about to fall over, out of air myself, Jack Purdy took a long and shuddering breath on his own.

"Good for you, mister," Ed said. She bent over him and called into his ear. "Now, breathe, you hear me?" Jack took another breath and then another, and a little color seeped into his face.

Ed told me to quit pressing and that we should turn him on his back. Then we both crouched over his face, watching as he came back to life. After a couple minutes he opened his eyes and looked straight up. "Sister," he said, "is that you?"

Ed jerked away, pulling her cap down over her face. "This here's Ed McGee," she grunted.

Jack was silent a long while except for the painful and wonderful sound of his breath going in and out. Finally, he asked, "Where am I?"

"You're on the gold rush trail," I told him, "and you darned near drowned dead in the Dyea River."

He tried to sit up but was weak as a cat and fell back. "I must've slipped on that bridge," he said slowly, as if he was working it out. "Lost my balance and fell facedown with a hundred-pound pack to keep me there." He was silent a while longer. "How'd you boys know?"

"I saw your red bandanna floating by," I said, "and wondered how come."

"Then you and a bandanna saved me, I guess." He took my hand and squeezed it tight. He wanted to grab Ed's hand, too, but she got up with a jerk.

"Come on, Billy," she said in her growly voice. "Let's see can we get his pack out of the river."

"You boys have done enough for me," Jack said. "I don't want to hold you up any more. That'd be poor payment for saving my life."

"Anybody on the trail would've done the same," I said.

"No sir, I don't believe they would. Some of these folks are in such a hurry to get to the gold fields, they wouldn't stop if their grandmas were drowning. I'm much obliged to you boys, truly. Please don't do any more."

But, of course, we did get his pack out of the water and opened up. Lucky, most of what he was carrying that day was gear and not food, although we found some soggy flapjacks, which we made him eat. Then, because he kept saying we had to get on our way, we left him sitting in a patch of sunshine, resting and mending his cut straps.

Ed clattered along the canyon trail fit to bust and didn't do more than grunt until we got all the way back to our last load. Then she let fly.

"You hear what he said, that fool, that Jack Purdy?"

"Huh?"

"He called me Sister, just like Pa does. You heard

that, didn't you? I must've been talking in my regular voice when we were saving his dratted life."

"Ed," I said, "he was as near dead as you can be and still come back. He didn't notice nothing, and won't recall it, if he did."

In the time we'd been on the gold rush trail, we'd seen plenty of folks of all ages and sizes, including women and children, and even babes in arms, or riding along in carts and wheelbarrows. Most of the women was wearing corsets and skirts just like they always did at home, going to church or cleaning house, even though that didn't seem like a good outfit for climbing mountains. But nobody was stopping them or even pointing them out.

"Anyways, it ain't going to matter to anyone if you're Ed or Edna Rose," I said.

"You are truly weak-minded, Billy McGee," she snapped, biting off each word. "You think the Mounties are going to let us into Canada if they know we're alone and I'm a female not even seventeen?"

"I don't know. I'm just saying I don't think it matters."

"Of course it matters, so keep your mouth shut, and don't go looking for trouble with Jack Purdy or nobody else, you hear me?"

"We saved his life, Ed. You call that looking for trouble?"

I guess I had her there, because the only answer she gave was to start loading our stuff into sacks, shoving and whacking things like they was giving her back talk.

For the rest of the day she set an awful pace through the canyon, and I didn't have much thought for anything but keeping going. There wasn't nobody at the log bridge or any sign of what had happened, except a trail of gravel caused by our sliding down the bank. When I crossed the bridge, being extra careful, I looked down into the rushing water and saw, in my mind's eye, him still lying there, face-down with his pinkish-colored hair all spread out and wavering in the Dyea River.

5

SHEEP CAMP

WHEN WE CAME TO SHEEP CAMP for the first time, I stopped dead and stared like a cheechako for sure. The camp was in what looked like a bowl scooped out from a ring of mountains. Away up northward, on a saddle between rocks and ice and snow, you could see a notch, like someone had dug out a chip with a penknife, the way Ma used to do with a spool of thread to keep the tail from unwinding. On the mountain it looked like a long string of black thread was wedged into the notch, its loose end hanging crooked against the slope and sort of quivering.

I was staring in wonderment when a man in a checkered cap happened by. He took his pipe out of his mouth and said, "Sonny, I see you have yet to be introduced to the sight of gold hunters doing the Chilkoot lockstep."

"I figured that's what it was," I said, not wanting to admit ignorance.

"Yes, sir," he said. "It's been that way almost day and night since the word got out about gold on the Klondike. Only time it slowed was during the mud-slide."

"Mudslide?"

"Yes sir. It came in the night after a heavy rain and poured right through here, carrying away tents and huts with folks asleep inside. Some was drowned."

Would Pa have been here then? "Do you know the names of the ones who was drowned?" I asked.

"Well, no, there weren't so many of them—two, three maybe. But plenty lost their outfits."

I could hardly breathe and still felt sick in my chest when I told Ed about the washout, but she said she knew already and I was only borrowing trouble, another habit of mine that was of no earthly use. "Pa is fine, don't you worry. We'd know if he wasn't."

"How would we know that, Ed?"

"I'd know. Now help me get the fire going to make our supper."

That's the way she had come to be. Except for the time we spent bringing Jack Purdy back to life, she didn't pay mind to anything but getting our stuff moved along. It was like something possessed her. If she wondered at the sight of that endless black thread being drawn over a notch in the Chilkoot Mountains, she never let on. It seemed she just couldn't entertain any possibility except that Pa would be waiting for us at Lake Bennett and then we would go on to the

Klondike and strike it rich. If she had any more thoughts than that, like how we was going to get on without our ma, she didn't say so but kept them under that squashed old hat.

I lost count of the days it took us to get everything up to Sheep Camp, which was the last place, folks said, where there was wood for campfires. In other ways, Sheep Camp was like Dyea or Skagway, only smaller and even more ragtag. Shacks and tents was scattered helter-skelter, with muddy lanes running between, and beyond them was the scraggly trees of the timberline and the great circle of mountains.

There was no reason for calling it Sheep Camp as far as I could tell. Horse Camp was more like it, because it was where you had to give up your horses, if you'd got them that far. Only two-legged animals could get themselves over the pass while carrying a load. Some horses belonged to packers who took them back to the sands of Dyea to start all over again, but others that was almost knackered was left to wander on their own, searching for a bit of grass to eat. They was pitiful to see.

A fair number of places in Sheep Camp were set up for business of one kind or another. One tent had a cross painted on it and was meant to be a church—Presbyterian, I think—with missionaries waiting for whoever wandered in. Another had a sign that said THE PALMER HOUSE and was run by a Mr. Palmer from Wisconsin. For five dollars you could get a bowl of stew—you wouldn't really be sure what the meat was—and a place on the floor to sleep, along with about forty other people. There was a crowd waiting to get in every night, and folks said Mr. Palmer didn't need to go no further to strike it rich, because he'd already found a gold mine.

In another tent was a piano that had been carted up the canyon, I don't know how. In the evenings you could hear it being played and some dance-hall women singing along, which sounded kind of pretty floating out through the night. I went and stood by the tent-flap door once. Inside, the women were flipping their skirts and showing off their legs as they hopped around between the makeshift benches. You could hardly hear the song for the men shouting and laughing. Some of them was gathered around little tables set up for card games and a roulette wheel. If you wanted a game of chance, you could find it in that tent, but there was plenty of other places for making wagers.

One man had a big book and a cane that turned out to have three legs, and the book wasn't a real book but a table that unfolded and sat on top of the cane. I had seen the man set up his table almost everywhere that folks stopped to rest, even at the side of the trail. He had walnut shells and a dried pea, which he made a great show of putting under one shell while everyone watched. Then he'd switch the shells around so fast, his hands blurred. Folks paid to guess which shell the pea was under. For a dozen times running, they'd be wrong and the man would keep their money, and then maybe one fellow would guess right and walk away looking smart. Funny thing was, I saw that very same man guess right at another place, and it looked like maybe he was in cahoots with the walnut-shell fellow. I thought folks'd get wise and warn others not to play, but pretty near always there was a little knot of people waiting to get cheated.

"Ain't it something," I said to Ed, "how folks keep on thinking they're gonna beat the game?"

"Most people are fools, Billy, counting on being lucky."

"But ain't that the same as us figuring on being lucky enough to strike it rich?"

"Not the same," she said. "We're working for our luck."

"That don't mean we're gonna get it."

"There you go, bellyaching again. Come on, it's time to turn in. We'll have another tough day tomorrow."

Of course, I wasn't bellyaching at all but merely pointing something out, as any fair-minded person would know—but that don't describe my sister, Ed.

Finally, the day came when we brought our last load into camp. If I had lost count of how many days it had taken us to shift our stuff, Ed had a tight grip on the matter. She figured if we put our minds to it and took on a little more than we had been carrying, we could get everything to the top of the pass in three or four days.

"You taken leave of your senses?" I asked. "We got to climb pretty near straight up from here on."

"But it's shorter, Billy. Only a few miles to the top. And we don't have time to spare if we want to catch up with Pa. Besides, the cold weather is coming on."

She was right about that. A feel of a change came every evening with the wind, and sometimes there was a skin of frost on our tent in the morning.

We spent half the next day dividing the outfit into piles, one for each trip. Then we made up two packs for the first climb.

"Put my pack on first," she ordered. "Then I'll do yours."

When I heaved the three canvas sacks she had lashed together onto her back, Ed made a little "oof" noise. She took a step forward and sunk slowly to the muddy ground. When I came around in front and saw her face, it almost made me laugh, except I knew better. She was so squashed, her cheeks looked like they went sideways. She could barely open her mouth to whisper, "Take some off."

I went around back, opened one of the bags, and took out some cooking pots.

"More," she said.

I took off one whole sack, unlashing all the cords she had put together so careful. When I looked again, her face was coming back round. Even so, I had to help her stand up.

"Well," she said, as though the whole notion of getting everything to the top so fast had been my idea, "no matter what you say, Indian packers can carry a lot more than we can. With all the practice they've had, it stands to reason."

There were Indian packers—Chilkat people, they was called, men and women and boys, too—who could hoist up a hundred pounds and start off walking steady and serious, as though it was just work. They didn't smile or say howdy or even act like they knew we was there, but just kept going. I admired them and wished we could ask them for help, or advice maybe. According to Ed, they charged a terrible amount of money. Seeing as we didn't have any money at all, there weren't no point in even thinking about getting help. So we divvied up the stuff again and made lighter loads.

There was only two places to stop for a rest before you joined the black thread wiggling its way up toward Chilkoot Pass. The first place was called Stone House, named for a huge boulder that made some shelter, and the second place was called the Scales, because everyone who had hired packers had to have all their stuff weighed over again and then pay more money to have it carried from there on. Ed didn't want to stop at either place, and insisted we keep going and test her idea of us making two trips a day.

"Come on, Billy. We can do this easy," she said while I stood shading my eyes against the fierce glare of snowfields and glaciers. "You remember how we went up Stocker's Hill back home? Like mountain goats, Pa said."

"But we wasn't carrying anything but berry buckets and sandwiches," I reminded her.

"I know you always look on the grim side, Billy, but I trust you ain't a coward."

That stung me pretty hard, just like she knew it would, and I trudged off without another word.

The trail got steeper and steeper until it was like climbing a hayloft ladder, easy enough when you was racing up to hide in the hay, but something else again with a fifty- or sixty-pound load. To make matters worse, on a trail nearby we could see folks who'd already reached the top and cached their gear skipping their way back down to Sheep Camp, with no loads on their backs and smiles on their faces, easy as pie.

There was no turning back, nor hardly any stopping to rest, neither. If you stepped off the trail, like as not you'd wait half a day before someone would let you back in line. I saw that soon enough and gritted my teeth to keep moving. Thinking hard thoughts about my sister helped, but then I must've begun to flag a little because she gave me a punch that I felt right through the pack.

"Cut it out, *Edna Rose,*" I said. That settled her hash for a while and gave me more energy for putting one foot in front of the other as we climbed what seemed like a granite wall. Sometimes I'd slip a little and have to dig my feet in sideways to keep my balance, but I never stepped out, not once. And by midafternoon I had crossed the pass a couple yards in front of my sister, Ed.

"Whoopee!" I yelled.

Seemed like I was standing on top of the world. In front was a trail heading down over stony slopes to the lakes that flowed into the Yukon River. Behind was the bowl where Sheep Camp lay, and beyond that the Dyea Canyon with its little river tumbling down to the sea. All around was walls of stone and ice. A glacier hung on one of them, with the sunlight flashing off it like a warning: *Watch your step.*

The Mounted Police had a post on the summit, no more than a tent cabin. You could see a table inside and a pile of ledgers. A couple Mounties stood guard on the downhill trail, making certain that no one went further without being written up in their record books and getting an okay from Canadian customs.

We had heard about that on the trail and knew to expect it. But no one had described what the top of the pass looked like, with all those stacks of goods. They was piled up neat for the most part, not like the beach at Dyea, but more like a little city of boxes and barrels and canvas bags. There was poles stuck in the ground beside some stacks, and I thought they was meant as street signs, like you should turn left at the pole with the coonskin tail and go straight on toward the one with a red rag. Someone told me later it was more to make sure people knew where to look for their outfits when a blizzard covered everything, as it might have done any day.

Me and Ed had to search around a while before we found a space for our stuff, but after we unloaded, I felt so light I practically floated off the ground. Even Ed forgot she was Ed for a minute and let out a happy yell. Then she remembered and jammed her hat further down on her head and said we couldn't rest for more than a few minutes.

We slid and jumped our way down a path made smooth by scores of others doing the same thing. Some folks sat on shovels and rode them back to Sheep Camp like sleds, whooping as they went. We went down so fast, the gold hunters shuffling and groaning on the way up disappeared in a blur. At the bottom we walked back into Sheep Camp and called it a day, or rather, Ed did. She was limping a little and thought she might have worked up a blister from wearing those outsize boots.

But the next morning she said she was cured and we should try for two trips. So we did, and after that kept it up pretty steady.

One morning we was halfway to the summit doing the ol' Chilkoot lockstep when something happened to stop us. I bumped up against Ed, and she against the fellow in front of her, and people piled up behind us, too. Muttering began to rise all along the line below, spiked with curses and then angry shouts. I leaned out a little to see what was the trouble. It seemed a fellow a few paces ahead had stopped—just straight-out halted in his tracks. I could see his bent-over shape and the wooden box he had strapped to his back. He swayed a little from side to side, but didn't take another step forward.

"Get him outta there!" someone shouted, and others took it up. Pretty soon the fellow was shoved off to the side. He slid backwards until he was right close to me, where there was a little level spot. Then he sunk down on his hands and knees with his load holding him down, pinned almost as good as Jack had been pinned down in the Dyea River, except this fellow could still breathe. The rest of us went on hauling ourselves upward.

Some hours afterward, when Ed and me were coming up with our second load of the day, I saw him again. He had gotten to his feet by then and was swaying under the weight of his box as he tried to worm his way back into line. His arms hung down, hands brushing against the slope, and he kept repeating, "Say, boys, would you give a man a break?" No one ahead of us even paused, and the fellow slithered downhill a little more until he was right by Ed.

"Say, young fella," he said. Ed kept her head bent over and pushed on by. She probably didn't even know I'd stopped until the grumbling took up behind me.

"Get in here, mister," I said, reaching out to grab one hanging arm. For a second it seemed he had forgot what he wanted and thought I might be attacking him. Then he understood and stumbled into place in front of me. I gave him a good push to get him going, and we all began again in the Chilkoot lockstep. There was some complaint behind me, but it died away. Everyone knew better than to waste their breath on something besides climbing.

That evening, while we was fixing our usual supper of beans and bacon back at Sheep Camp, Ed began to jaw at me.

"I swear, Billy, you can't seem to get it in your head that our job is to get to Pa as quick as we can. You got no business giving some stranger a place ahead of you and using up strength which you ain't got much to spare of."

"Ma didn't raise us to ignore other folks' troubles," I said, "nor Pa, neither."

Her eyes hardened. "They didn't raise us to be fools, Billy McGee."

"I suppose you think I should've left that fellow to freeze there, or maybe even give him a kick downhill? And I suppose we shouldn't have wasted our time saving Jack Purdy from drowning dead."

She stirred the beans round and round with a blue-speckled enamel spoon that had belonged to Ma. "Folks ain't always so all-fired grateful when you do something for 'em, Billy. They're out for theirselves first and last, and wonder what's the matter with you if you ain't, and maybe treat you shabby, too, because of it. Before this trek is over, you'll see I'm right. Now, get your plate. I'm ready to ladle out these beans."

I knew something was cuckoo in her notion. But since I was near starved and couldn't stand any more jawing, I let it go.

6

THE TOP OF THE WORLD

THE DAY CAME when we had only one more load to carry to the top of Chilkoot Pass. I hopped around our last breakfast fire in Sheep Camp feeling pretty frisky. "By nightfall we'll be on the downhill trail to Lake Bennett and Pa," I said.

"First we got to get by the Mounties," Ed replied with a grim look. She had padded herself extra thick with clothes and rubbed a fresh handful of dirt over her face. Her hair had grown out a little, so she tamed it flat with bacon grease before putting on the old hat.

She had worked out our story, too, and drilled me until I had it by heart. We were brothers, Ed and Bill McGee, eighteen and sixteen, on our way to join our pa and his partners at Lake Bennett.

"You do most of the talking, Billy, like I'm one of those fellows that hardly speak. You know the kind. I'll throw in a word now and then."

"Sure, Ed, sure." I knew I was a little runty to be taken for sixteen, and Ed made a peculiar sort of fellow, but I didn't think it was going to matter anyhow. I was certain that Ed and me would slip by, no matter what our story.

We had to take our tent and bedrolls along with some other stuff on that trip, making a heavy load, but knowing it was the last one over Chilkoot helped ease the pain.

On top we spent time getting our gear stacked neat for the Mounties to inspect and then waited in line at the customs tent. The Mounties had big ledger books they carried around. When it came your turn, the officer you got would take a ledger and follow you to your cache to check it.

While we was waiting, we watched one of the officers checking through a nearby stack of goods. He rolled out a barrel that was labeled APPLES and made the man, a rabbity-looking fellow, pry it open. Inside was a few apples . . . and below that a smaller barrel of whiskey. My, did that put the officer in a bad mood. The rabbity man was supposed to pay customs duties but didn't have any money, so he was required to pour his whiskey out on the stony ground. Then the Mountie made him open every other sack and bag and bundle to make sure there wasn't no more stuff to pay customs on. By the time that officer got to us, he was pretty brisk.

"Afternoon, sir," I said, tugging at my cap brim.

"Names and places of birth," he said, pronouncing his words like a schoolteacher or maybe a judge.

"William Gipson McGee here, and that's Edwin Ross McGee there." I pointed at my sister, who was standing a little way off with her hat brim pulled down. "We're brothers, born in the state of Washington, near Chehalis, if you know where that is, sir."

"How old are you?"

"I'm sixteen and my brother is eighteen."

The Mountie gave Ed a closer look. "Dates of birth?"

"April 15, 1879," she growled without a second's delay. Had it all ready, and so did I.

"January 3, 1881, sir."

"They must send boys to seek their fortunes a bit early in the state of Washington. I don't believe you've ever had to shave, have you, Mr. William McGee?"

"Being slow that way runs in our family," I said. "But we catch up. Our uncle Peter has a beard halfway to his bellybutton." This was only a small exaggeration that I threw in, but Ed jerked her shoulder at me, and I could tell that she didn't want no ornaments to the story.

"This pile of goods is yours, I assume, Mr. McGee?"

"You bet. Manhandled all the way from Dyea, sir."

He had us hold up bags and bundles and say what was inside, and some of them he opened and looked for himself. This took a little while, but everything seemed to be going along all right, until he got out his ledger and asked, "Now, then, which one of you is going on to Lake Bennett?"

"Both of us, sir. We're both going," I said, after a little pause.

"Then where is the second outfit?"

Ed had moved off to one side, but I could tell without even looking that she had stiffened. Me, I was so stunned, I couldn't hardly think.

"This is more than enough for Ed and me, sir," I stuttered. "This'll do us fine."

The Mountie sighed. "I thought all you treasure seekers had been forewarned at Dyea that Her Majesty's government requires each one of you to have enough supplies to last for an entire year. Otherwise, you cannot cross the Canadian border, which is right here under our feet."

"We don't eat a lot," I said.

That didn't seem like a good answer. The officer closed his book. "What you have here is barely enough for one person. Therefore, only one of you can go on. Do you understand?"

"We understand we're going on together," Ed burst out. "Our pa is waiting for us, and he's a U.S. citizen, mister." It was the most she had said to anyone except me since we left Skagway, and she had trouble keeping her voice pitched low for the whole speech. The Mountie swung around and faced her.

"He may well be, but that has nothing to do with the matter. You're on Canadian soil now, and these are Canadian rules. When you decide which one is going on, I'll record his name, or the two of you can turn around and go back, whichever you wish."

"Please, sir, we got to stay together and go on to find our pa. He's waiting for us, sir," I said.

"The law is the law." The officer closed his book. That must've been the last straw for Ed. She flung down the bag of goods she'd been holding and started for him with her head down, as if she had a mind to butt him off the mountaintop. He gaped in astonishment at the sawed-off person coming at him, fists swinging. I froze, with awful thoughts coursing through my mind. In a second she'd wham into him, probably screeching in her own voice; then she'd be put under arrest for whacking an officer of the Royal Mounted Police and traveling under a false name. We'd never see our pa again.

The officer said, "Here, now," and dodged to one side so Ed had to change direction. In that instant, someone grabbed her from behind.

"Whoa there, Ed," the person said. "What's going on?"

It was Jack Purdy come up out of nowhere, his pale hair gleaming in the afternoon sun like a lighted pine knot. Ed struggled against his grip, but didn't speak.

"The officer says our outfit ain't big enough for two people," I explained. "One of us has to go back to Dyea, according to him."

Jack swung Ed around and looked at me over her shoulder. "Why, Bill," he said, "didn't you tell him that some of our goods has gone forward already?"

The officer had got hold of his balance. He brushed off his uniform and straightened his brown peaked hat, then patted it a couple times, giving him a moment to adjust to this new story, I supposed. He pointed out how serious it was to threaten an officer of Her Majesty's police.

"Oh, yes, sir," Jack said, "and we apologize, don't we, Ed?" He shook her a little. "These boys are just wore out with getting up the hill and don't have all their wits about 'em in this thin air in Canada."

"Be that as it may, they still don't have enough food for two people."

"Well, sir, the main part of our party went to Lake Bennett earlier on, and they were carrying some of our stuff. Ain't that so, boys?"

"Sure," I said. "Pa and his partners went ahead."

"And the reason for that," Jack went on, smooth as butter, "was that Ed here went down with the fever. You know, sir, it's been taking a toll in Dyea, and the two of us stayed behind to nurse him back to health. He's still a little poorly, as you can tell, sir." Jack turned Ed loose, and she wobbled around, still furious but not too stunned to miss what was going on.

"Not lacking in energy, I see," the Mountie said coolly. "However, if what you say is the case, you should have told me earlier. If your father came across this pass in the past few weeks, his name will be in our customs register. What would you estimate the date of crossing to be, Mr. McGee?"

I didn't know which one he meant and didn't have

no idea how to answer, but Ed did, which showed she was not cuckoo, although she had acted like it. "Middle of August, most likely," she said in her Ed voice.

"Very well. Let's go see."

The officer led us back to the customs tent and got out another book, which he laid on a table, then went through page by page with Ed and me looking on. And there it was, I could tell, even upside down, Gipson McGee, because Pa made great big peaks out of the M in McGee. It was August 16, 1897. The officer seemed a little disappointed to see that our story was holding together. He pointed out that there was no notation about any others coming along later and no indication that the McGee party was carrying extra rations, either.

"But I know they were, sir," Jack said. "I'll vouch for it, having helped 'em pack. And you know, too, sir, that when a person has extra, you don't mark that down, like you didn't with me."

"Yes," the officer said, "I recall clearing you yesterday. Isn't it odd you three weren't traveling together?"

"My thoughts exactly," Jack said. "I been hanging around here all day waiting for you boys. Where the dickens have you been?" He began to jaw at us like that. Ed glowered while I run through a couple of stories, explaining. In the middle of this, the officer finally said he'd let us go, although it was against his better judgment. Somehow we got our names signed in the book and ourselves out of that tent and back to our pile of goods. It was such a close call, I didn't even feel like dancing a jig or whooping.

"I don't know how to thank you, Jack," I said.

"It's nothing compared to what you boys did for me back in Dyea Canyon."

"Ah, no," I said, "that's all right, Jack."

No one spoke for a minute or so while we stared at the ground and then up at the afternoon sky.

"Are you going right on?" I asked finally.

"I aim to. I've got a sort of sledge I carried on my back over the pass, and I plan to load it with my outfit and drag it down to Lake Bennett. But you know, I could use an extra hand to help me haul." He paused for a second and glanced at Ed. "What do you say the three of us throw in together from here to the lake? We could relay our stuff a lot faster that way."

It seemed too good to be true. "That'd be great, Jack," I said. "With the three of us and the sledge, we can probably move our outfits in jig time. What do you say, Ed?"

My sister glared at me, and I could tell she was scrabbling through her mind for some reason to refuse, a reason that wouldn't look pure foolish, since what he was offering would get us to Lake Bennett and Pa faster and she knew it. Finally, she pulled her hat brim down over her eyes and shrugged.

"All right," she said, "but just to the lake."

After that she would hardly speak to me, never mind Jack. In fact, for the next few days she was as sore as a boiled owl, as Ma used to say, and didn't try to hide it, neither.

7

DOWNHILL TO LAKE BENNETT

AFTER WE CROSSED INTO CANADA, the landscape looked different. There were patches of marshy grass, but mostly the land was barren rock, with not much in the way of bushes or trees until further down. The trail was broader and the traveling somewhat easier, especially with Jack's sledge to carry the heavy sacks—although it took a good deal of hauling and shoving to keep it going in the right direction. Still, with the three of us shifting two outfits, we moved along at a pretty good clip.

Jack and me talked and traded stories while we walked, taking turns pulling or guiding the sledge. I told him some of the stories from the book that Tom Thunder had taken, mostly so I would remember them myself, and he told stories he had picked up on his travels. He didn't seem to have a home or family that he wanted to speak about and didn't mention the sister that he had mistook Ed for. Ed did her part with the sledge, but wouldn't talk except to growl. If it wasn't her turn to push or guide, she charged ahead almost out of sight. The first night Jack cooked supper, dried potatoes with a little bacon, and she refused to eat, although later I caught sight of her rummaging through a sack of dried fruit. After that, she ate when we did, but took her food and sat off at a distance. Jack and me played cards by the fire those nights, and Ed would go sit on a rock a few paces away until it got pitch-dark, and then she would crawl into her blanket roll without another word. She kept her hat on day and night so far as I knew, and when she had to relieve herself on the trail, she hiked a long way off to make certain no one could see her. It must've been kind of hard to keep up the game, but Ed was nothing if not stubborn.

When we had all been together, Ma and Pa and my sister and me, she had been famous for getting hopping mad when things didn't turn out to her satisfaction, like the time she baked the applesauce cake for Pa's birthday. It rose lopsided, and she declared it was my fault for tromping around the kitchen when the cake was in the oven. She worked herself into such a fit that when Pa came home and said it wasn't bad for a landscape, complete with hills and valleys, she took the cake, still warm from the oven, trotted it outside, and flung it in the chicken coop. We didn't have much extra in the way of eggs and butter then, and Ma was stunned.

"Edna Rose, honey, you got a definite bent toward cutting off your nose to spite your face," she said, while we stared at the chickens having a feast of cake. Edna went into such serious sulking I thought she'd set a record, but this here on the gold rush trail threatened to outdo that. I truly didn't understand the point of it. We had got by the Mounties, we was moving faster than before, and we was more likely to actually find Pa, but that didn't seem to make things better for Ed. Seemed she had something stuck in her craw, and a couple days after Chilkoot was when she choked on it.

We'd had our supper, and me and Jack was playing Seven Up by the fire. Where we was camped you could see a great rock wall to the west with a jagged top. After the sun slipped down, it left a glowing rim along the ragged edge of rock.

"See that light there?" Jack said. "That's most likely where trolls will gather, if they have trolls in this country, which I don't doubt."

"What's trolls, Jack?"

"Sawed-off mountain folk, Billy, kin to goblins. My grandma came from Finland, where folks believe in trolls living in the mountains and coming down now and then to make mischief. These are just the right kind of mountains, too." He gave me a sideways look, and I wasn't quite sure whether he was fooling or not.

"What kind of mischief, Jack?"

"They spoil your milk, or fix it so the butter won't churn, or make the hens quit laying. Sometimes they move into your house and eat everything in the cupboards."

"We don't have hens or milk or a house, neither, Jack, so I guess we're okay."

"Oh, I don't know about that. They might find some other way to get us," Jack said.

At that, Ed, who'd been sitting off a ways like she didn't know us, got up and came sauntering over to the fire.

"Deal me in, if you don't mind," she said in her Ed voice.

Jack glanced up at her. "Sure thing, Ed." He gathered the cards, shuffled, and dealt them out again.

Ed fanned out her cards and took the first turn without even asking. We played along for a couple rounds. Then she said, "It don't seem very friendly for you to be terrifying my little brother, Mr. Purdy."

My mouth dropped open. "What are you jawing about, Ed?"

"All them troll stories will give him bad dreams. He's always been a baby about scary tales."

"Am not," I said. "And I ain't such a baby as to believe trolls are real."

Jack was watching Ed pretty close. "Well," he said, "according to my grandma they are, or used to be—them and the little folk, too. I like to keep my eye out for any of that sort, just in case."

It was Ed's turn to play, but she just studied her cards. "Well, then, mister, you can be the one to pat my little brother on the shoulder when he wakes up bawling."

"I won't wake up bawling about trolls," I yelled, near to choking. "That's a blamed lie!"

"Is it?" Ed went on fanning through her cards and shifting them around. Then she laid down a card and won the round. "It's your turn to deal, little brother, if you can stop whining long enough to play."

The game was ruined for me, of course, the game and the whole blamed evening, but I couldn't stop myself from trying to make Ed admit that I never woke up bawling about ghosts and trolls. The more I tried, the calmer she got, until what happened was that tears actually did come into my eyes and my voice went bad.

"See?" she said, nodding at Jack. "I told you he was a crybaby."

I jumped at her and tried to jerk off her hat, but she got a good grip on it, and we tussled back and fore until Jack pulled me aside.

"Here, here," he said. "Take it easy, cap'n."

"That ain't my name!" I yelled. "And Ed ain't his, neither." But for some reason I couldn't tell on her, not even after what she said. Too cowardly, I told myself, as I got out my bedroll and took it far off, like Ed usually did. I lay on the lumpy ground and thought what could I do to pay her back. It just wasn't fair. I had done pretty much all she wanted since we left Skagway, and here she was, shaming me in front of Jack for no reason I could see.

After a long time, when nearly all the muttering and sounds from other camps had died away and stars was shining in the clear, cold night, I heard the sound of footsteps and felt someone crouching by my side. I turned my head away.

"You'd better come closer to the fire, Billy," Ed said in her regular voice. "I fixed a place for you."

"No thanks. I wouldn't want to be anywhere near a liar."

She sighed. "I'm sorry, Billy. I didn't know you'd take it so hard."

That was such a stupid remark, I wouldn't give her the satisfaction of an answer.

Then she said, "Sometimes you act like you're the only one in the family who has any feelings."

"Yeah," I said, "that's right. Me and Ma."

Ed made a noise like she was sucking her breath through her teeth. "She was my mother, too, you know," she said. Then she got up and went away before I could think of an answer.

The next morning we all set to work as usual, and nobody remarked on what had happened around the fire the night before. From then on, Ed didn't keep to herself so much and would eat with us and clean up when it was her turn, but she still hardly had a word to say.

I could see Jack eyeing her now and again, like he didn't know what to make of that person, but when he sent a comment her way, she wouldn't answer or gave only a word or two in her Ed growl. Then he'd cut a grin at me, but I wasn't having any of that. The trouble was partly his fault—him and his troll stories. Still, I couldn't help wanting to hear more of those, so I was in a pickle, trudging along, hauling that sledge, thinking first one way and then another, and wanting to talk to Jack, but not doing it.

I turned my mind to Pa, and how surprised he would be to see us, and if I should lay charges against my sister—for what I wasn't quite sure, but I was hoping Pa would come down on her when we found him, if we ever did.

We was going downhill pretty steady then, and there was time to look around at the strange country we had come into, different from the Dyea Valley and the mountain pass. There was hundreds of little ponds amongst the rocks, with dark water reflecting the sky and clouds at midday. When we came down lower, there was real trees—lodgepole pine and fir—but mostly stunted and scrubby. The air was chilly, early and late, and there'd be a sprinkling of frost on the mossy grass when you crawled out in the mornings. It was the feel of winter sneaking up on us.

We passed Lake Lindeman, where some folks were building boats, but we didn't find Pa there, and everyone advised going on to the bigger camp at Lake Bennett. On the fourth day below Chilkoot we came up over a rise, and there it was, dark shining water stretching north between mountains that looked like prime places for trolls, although nobody mentioned that. Pretty soon you could see the shore dotted with tents and hear the sounds of chopping and sawing as folks worked on their boats. A few them were already out on the lake, slowly moving north toward the Yukon River.

8

LOOKING FOR A MAN IN A MACKINAW JACKET

PA MIGHT BE in one of those boats, I thought, *floating away from us right while we stand here watching.* "Let's go," I said, jerking as hard as I could on the sledge rope.

"Easy," Jack said. "We won't get there any sooner by knocking our outfits into the gully. You and Ed go on, find a place to cache the stuff, and I'll catch up with you later."

I didn't need a second invitation, but set off trotting with Ed behind me. We reached the south shore about noontime and marked a lookout place for Jack to stash the goods. Then we agreed Ed would go one way around the head of the lake and I would go the other. We'd meet back at the cache by sunset.

At first I felt so filled with hope that I almost skipped from one group of folks to the next, asking for news of Gipson McGee and his partners. But after several hours of crisscrossing back and forth between tents and half-built boats, I began to flag a little. Most of the men who weren't hacking down trees was trying to turn logs into planks, a proposition that appeared to cause a good deal of argument. It was like walking into a thicket of snarls and curses just to get close enough to ask anyone a question. And even then I had to be ready to dodge off pretty quick.

"McGee, Tanner, and Black," I'd say. "My pa—that would be Gipson McGee, but some folks call him Gip—has a big brown mustache, kind of droopy, and he wears a black hat and a brand-new mackinaw jacket. Leastways, it was new when he left Skagway." Ma had made him get that jacket, taking money meant for food, and he had gone off proud as anything.

The people who listened to me sometimes gave it a little thought, but the answer was always the same. "Well, kid, that describes about half the men on the trail, mackinaw jacket and all, but the name don't mean anything to me. How about the rest of you slackers?" And the others would shake their heads, if they even bothered to do that, and go back to whipsawing or hammering.

By late afternoon I had worked my way around my side of the lake to where the clusters of tents thinned out, and I was getting low in spirits, barely holding on to the hope that Ed might have had better luck. The sun was moving toward the western ridge when I came across three men, not whipsawing or building but seeming to be at war with a piece of battered canvas they was attempting to turn into a sail.

When I put my question, one of them paused in his rassling. "That sounds about right for that party we met on the trail from Lake Lindeman, don't it, boys?"

A second man grunted, "I saw 'em again a couple days back on the deck of one of them big rafts. They're well downriver by now—if they didn't drown in Miles Canyon."

I blinked hard. "You certain, mister?"

"Well, I'll tell ya, it didn't look like their pilot knew much about boating. I wouldn't be surprised if they capsized."

"Shut your trap, Al," another said. "That ain't no way to talk to a young fella about his pa."

"Who ya tellin' to shut up?"

"You, that's who. Can't ya see the kid's near broke up?"

I turned away from them and stared out at the lake, blinking back tears. For once it looked like I was right and Ed was wrong. We had missed Pa after all.

Behind me the two fellows kept on snarling at each other, until there was a sudden sound like a shot. I whirled around and saw the third man rise up and snap the canvas again, like a bed sheet straight off the clothesline.

"Stop your yammerin', both of you," he said, and then came over and laid a hand on my shoulder. "That party did set sail two, three days back, but the one in the red jacket must've missed the boat. He had got some bad news, I heard, and stayed behind. I saw him yesterday."

He was grimy and sunburnt, his beard speckled with food and sawdust, and his hat was pulled down around his ears, but he looked like an angel to me and I came close to throwing my arms around him.

"Where, mister, where?"

He gestured. "Back yonder, sonny, where all the commerce is—the hotels and supply places."

I began to run even before he finished and just barely had enough wit to throw a "Much obliged" over my shoulder.

It seemed a long way back, even though I was running at full tilt. When I came into the main cluster of tents, I saw that one of them had HOTEL printed on a slab outside. A man standing guard there listened to my description and shook his head. There was no one like that at the hotel, but I might try a place further on where they rented sleeping space. He pointed down a rutted lane to where a woman was sitting on a stool, peeling potatoes. I ran over to her and repeated my description. She gave me a narrow-eyed look and gestured with her knife toward the lake.

"Try that fella, sonny."

A man was sitting on the top log of a saw-pit frame, not doing anything, just sitting hunched over, his hands on either side to keep him from rolling off. With the setting sun in my eyes, I couldn't see the color of his jacket, but I was pretty sure who it was. "Pa!" I yelled. "Is that you?"

At first he didn't seem to take notice, only kept staring at the ground, and when he did look up, it was toward the mountains behind me instead of where I was coming along, suddenly feeling kinda shy somehow.

"Pa, it's me, Billy."

"Billy's not here," he said.

I had reached him by then and tugged at his boot. "Yes, I am, Pa. Down here. Look."

"My family's broke up," he said, still staring off like I was a stranger asking his story.

"No, Pa, I'm right here at Lake Bennett, and so is Edna Rose, only she calls herself Ed now. We come to find you, Pa."

He gripped the log platform and squinted down at me. "Where's your ma?"

I swallowed hard. "She died back in Skagway a few weeks ago."

"I heard that story, but I can't seem to take it in." Then he looked down again, and his face shifted, like it had just come to him who I was. He made a hoarse cry, "Billy, Billy," then jumped down and grabbed me, holding me a long time against the mackinaw jacket, which smelled of sawdust and sweat.

"How can it be that your ma is gone?" he said finally.

"I don't know, Pa. She got a fever and couldn't seem to hang on."

"Ah," he said, "Rose Ellen, my honey." He gripped me and rocked back and forth. I didn't know whether he was crying or it could've been me.

"How's you get here?" he asked after a time.

"We hoofed it, Pa."

He was silent awhile, still holding me. "Well," he said at last, "I guess you must've, but I can't take it in. Where's your sister?"

"Looking for you, if she ain't back at our meeting place."

"Then let's go there, son." He kept his arm around me as we walked back up the trail, and every little while he would grip me tight again. "The news just about broke my heart. She was fine and hearty when I left, or I never would've gone. You know that, son."

"Sure, Pa. I don't guess anyone could've stopped what happened." I looked up at him. "The neighbors took up a collection to bury her, but there wasn't enough for a gravestone."

I wanted to tell him how Ma lay there that afternoon, her eyes following me around, like she wanted something, I didn't know what. When I asked, *Ma, what can I do?* she opened her mouth, but no words came out. I'd been waiting to tell someone that. But it seemed like I couldn't, so I swallowed it down and figured to tell about Edna Rose instead, how she'd turned into Ed and wore men's clothes.

"After Ma died, Edna Rose took it into her head we had to find you."

"Now that you're here, son, I ain't going to chide you, but it was a dangerous thing for you and Sister to take on."

"And she ain't my sister anymore."

"Huh?" he said, stopping straight on the trail and looking scared. "Don't tell me something's gone wrong with Sister?"

"You might say that," I said, wondering if Pa would stop calling her Sister like he always done, once he saw the turn she had took, "and you might not."

He gripped me hard. "Is she hurt or ailing?"

"No, Pa, not exactly. Though it could be she's ailing, the way she acts. She hoofed it right along with me over Chilkoot Pass, and I thought it was on account of the Mounties that she called herself Ed, but then she wouldn't give it over and has to talk funny all the time around Jack, which don't make sense."

"You don't make sense yourself, son," he said.

Just then I looked up and saw my sister standing on the lookout rock where we had left our stuff, and she saw us, too. She leaped down and came running as fast as she could in those boots that didn't fit.

"Pa, Pa!" she screeched, and flung herself right on him. For a second he staggered backward, wondering who this strange fellow was, I supposed.

"Sister," he said finally, "that ain't you, is it? My daughter, Edna Rose?"

"Yes, Pa, it's me." She tore off the old hat, and there was her spiky, greasy hair going every which way and her cheeks dirty like she always kept 'em so folks wouldn't know she lacked a beard. They stared at each other, and then he folded her in his arms and rocked her back and fore like he'd done to me. I guessed they was both sniffling, so I walked on a bit and saw Jack had come up with the sledge and was watching the whole thing. When Pa and Ed walked up to the lookout place, I said, "This is Jack Purdy, who got us by the Mounties, Pa."

"That so?" Pa said. "Then I'm much obliged," and stuck out his hand after he got untangled from Edna Rose. Of course, she wanted to tell what happened, but I hopped in first and gave Jack full credit for Chilkoot Pass and from then on with his sledge.

If Jack was surprised about Edna Rose, he didn't show it, except to say he was glad to hear the rightful owner of the voice that had brought him up out of drowning. Ed's face went red, and then Pa had to know what he was talking about.

"Your kids, Mr. McGee, saved my life when I tumbled into the Dyea River. I owe 'em a debt for that and more," Jack said.

Then we had to tell the whole tale, me and Edna Rose fighting to say whatever came next, and Pa said, "Whoa now, I want to hear every word, twice over, but we can do that at supper. I got some fresh fish laid aside, and I'll bet you got the makings for biscuits."

It was clear he meant for Jack to come along and easy to see that wasn't to Ed's liking. But she was so happy about finding Pa, she put up with it—maybe glad enough to talk without growling at last.

While we was eating, Pa asked Jack where he had come from in Wisconsin, and how he got this far, and was he on his own?

"Yes, sir," Jack said. "I had a partner I met up with in Seattle, but he turned back when we got to Dyea."

"What about your folks?"

Jack shook his head. "I don't have much in the way of folks, Mr. McGee." Then he added, "Life was pretty tough for farmers back there when the banks failed. Folks lost everything they had, and some of 'em just gave up."

"So I heard," Pa said. "Same out in Washington State, when the lumber mills closed down."

"We wouldn't have come this far without Jack," I said into the silence of everyone thinking about hard times. "Me and Ed would still be on top of Chilkoot Pass arguing with the Canada Mounties."

"And I'd be laying in the Dyea River," Jack said.

"Well, well, it's a rare wind that don't blow somebody good somewhere along the line," Pa said.

We was all quiet for a time except for the clatter of spoons on our tin plates as we scraped up the last bits of fish and biscuit. Then Jack stood up, saying there was another load of provisions at our meeting place and he had a mind to haul it down while there was still some light, and no, he didn't need help, thanks.

That left us three together. Pa put one arm around

me and the other around my sister. "I got my family," he said softly. "What there is left of it without your ma, anyhow. So, now what do we do?"

"Why, Pa, surely we go on to the Klondike," Ed said, hardly taking a breath.

"It's getting late in the year, Sister. Looked like snow a couple days back, and there's no telling when the lake and river will freeze up. They say it takes a long while to get to Dawson at the best of times."

"We can do it, Pa. We got this far, didn't we?"

"You surely did, and I'm proud of you, but it may be more than a notion going down the Yukon River at the edge of winter. Some folks are going to stay over to finish their boats and go in the spring."

"But, Pa, that'll be too late. All the good claims will likely be gone by then."

"I'm none too sure about risking my family skippering a boat when I don't know beans about it."

"Jack does," I said. "He grew up where there's lots of lakes. Told me he learned to handle a boat early on."

"That so?" Pa said. "Well, now, that puts a different color on it."

Ed grabbed at his arm. "Oh, Pa," she said, "please don't bring him into it. This is just us McGees, going gold hunting. He ain't family."

"Neither were those men I was partners with."

That stopped her for just a second. "But you didn't have Billy and me then, Pa. We're better than partners because we're your family."

"I won't agree to go on to Dawson just me and my two kids. Your ma wouldn't hold with that."

"But she wouldn't want us to give up."

"No," he said, "I guess not. But she wouldn't want us to be foolhardy, neither."

"Why should we trust a stranger, Pa?"

"Looks like we'll have to, unless you want to turn tail and go home," Pa replied, poking at the fire. "Though to be honest, I don't know where that would be."

"Billy," Ed said, giving me a pleading look, "you don't want a stranger tagging along, do you?"

Well, she ought to 've known better than look to me for help after calling me a crybaby in front of Jack Purdy, not to mention bossing me the whole time. So I said, real careful, to Pa, "You think that with Jack's help we can build a boat and get to Dawson before freeze-up?"

"Don't know, Billy. Maybe. Anyway, we'll need an agreement about Jack being a partner before we talk boat building."

Tell the truth, I didn't have no notion of what we'd do after we found Pa, but now this idea of sailing downriver with my friend Jack seemed pretty good. "I'm agreed," I said.

"And you, Sister?"

Ed scraped our tin plates into the fire so fierce, fish bones and biscuit crumbs went flying. "Oh, all right," she said finally, "but only for going downriver. When we get to Dawson, he'll have to go his own way."

"Maybe Jack won't agree," Pa said. "We ain't got much to recommend us."

"And another thing, Pa—I ain't doing all the cooking and cleaning for you three."

"I'm willing to do my full share," came a voice. It was Jack, who must've halted the sledge a ways off and come up quiet.

My sister whirled around. "McGees don't take to being spied on, mister," she snapped.

"Beg pardon, miss," Jack said, and held out his hand. My sister acted like she didn't see it and went on whacking the plates and the frying pan. Funny thing, after saying she wasn't going to clean up, that's exactly what she did. Then Pa said we all had to shake hands on our partnership.

Jack took her hand and said, "I don't know what to call you, miss."

Well, that got her, you can bet. She didn't say anything for a moment, then she flung her head up and said, "You can refer to me as Miz McGee."

I had to snort laughing, and even Pa smiled.

"All right," said Jack, "Miz McGee it is." Then we all shook hands like Pa required and laid out our bedrolls.

Even with her hat off, the name Edna Rose still didn't seem to suit my sister anymore. Miz McGee didn't, neither, but that was Jack's lookout. Pa went on calling her Sister, like he always done. But for me she had turned into Ed, and it seemed like she was going to stay that way.

9

ON THE RIVER

THE NEXT MORNING Pa had a surprise for us. He led us a little way beyond the saw pit toward the lakeshore, where there was a tent all pegged down. He pulled up a couple pegs, and we saw inside a half-finished scow. Seemed him and his partners had got that far when he heard about Ma.

"I lost heart," he said. "Couldn't seem to go forward or back, and they couldn't wait, for fear of not getting to the Klondike this year. Partnered out with another group and left me with this to pay off my share of the tools and such. Thought I'd sell it, but didn't have enough gumption yet." He patted the planks. "It's not a great piece of construction, but might be seaworthy. What do you think, Jack?"

Jack went all around the boat, looking very closely, and said it would likely float, with a little more work and a lot of caulking.

The work meant making a few more planks and searching the slopes for a lodgepole pine, tall and slim enough to make the mast. That was left up to me and Ed while Pa and Jack went to whipsawing planks, the job that had made more enemies out of friends than you could shake a stick at, Pa told us. The log to be sawed into planks was laid on top of the platform lengthwise and marked as straight as possible with a cut line. That was for the two-handled saw with its mean-looking teeth. One fellow stood on top, guiding the saw along the marked line, while the fellow below did most of the heavy work, pulling the saw down through green wood, at the same time filling his eyes with sawdust and his ears with complaints about him not pulling hard enough. Likely he yelled back, if he had any breath left, that the top fellow wasn't guiding the saw right or that he was straight-out holding on to it, to make the bottom work impossible. Pa said some quarrels had got so fierce that men who had been friends all their born days and sworn to defend one another against all comers would turn into bitter enemies. There was a story going around of two such gold hunters, who made sure their partnership was split forever by sawing all their goods in half, including sacks of flour.

Pa and Jack didn't have trouble that way, maybe because they hardly knew each other. Mostly they just sawed and grunted and then changed places. I helped guide the saw from the top sometimes and so did Ed, except she refused to work with Jack, so I got to when he was below. In spite of being on the short side and wiry, he had good strength in his arms and shoulders and could even put Pa to shame, hauling that saw down through the green wood.

In a few days there was enough to finish the scow, which we did, following Pa's instructions. All the time we was watching over our shoulders for changes in the weather. First thing every morning we'd run down to the shore to see if new ice had come in the night. We was well into September by then, and folks who knew the country said there was little hope of getting to Dawson that late. Still, some people were determined to try, us among them.

When the scow was just about finished, Pa called us together. "Another day, and we'll be ready to launch. I just want to make sure once more that we're all agreed to do this thing."

We all agreed and shook hands. "You're not going to go back on that, are you, Pa?" Ed said so sharp that I looked to Pa to see if he weren't going to task her for taking that tone with him.

But he just gave her a look and went on. "I'm only making sure everyone is still agreed. I know where you stand, Sister." He turned to me. "What about you, Billy?"

"Sure, Pa. We can try, anyway," I said, for the pure reason I didn't have no other plan in mind.

Pa turned to Jack. "What do you say?"

"Well, Mr. McGee," he said, "I'm inclined to go along with your young'uns. According to what I hear up and down the shore, if we stay, we'll be stuck seven, eight months, living off our grub with no chance of staking a claim until next summer. And it looks like by spring there'll be a real crowd here, jostling cheek by jowl and filling up the lake."

"That's probably so," Pa said. "But if we're only partway to the Klondike at freeze-up, this boat won't do us any good, and we'll be trapped for the rest of the winter wherever that place is."

"What's the point of worrying about that now, Pa?" Ed said. "Let's just get going." She had eased her tone a little, but I could see the fear of being balked twitching at her.

Jack said, "I been thinking, Mr. McGee—we might look around and see if we can acquire some strips of metal that I could hammer into runners. Then we could tear up the boat and make it into a sled, if need be."

"You talking about hauling two tons of supplies for maybe a couple a hundred miles, Jack?"

"Folks tell me it's been done."

"We might freeze in our tracks."

"That's true, we might."

We was all quiet, except for the rustle Ed was making to keep from bursting out.

Finally, Pa sighed. "All right, but if we aren't past

Lake LaBarge before freeze-up, you'll all have to agree to come back here. Are we agreed?"

We were agreed.

Next day we launched our scow and put up the sail that me and Ed had made out of tent canvas, and we went sailing down Lake Bennett, headed for the Yukon River.

Jack did know a good deal about boating, and with him at the steer board we went along pretty easy, until near Miles Canyon with its rapids and whirlpool. Then Pa announced that he and Jack had talked to Sergeant Steele of the Mounties about the dangers of capsizing and had decided that the two of them would take our scow through the rapids alone.

"What do you mean, alone?" Ed asked.

"I mean that you and Billy will take some of our goods and Jack's sledge and portage around. There's a clear trail, they say. We'll pick you up further down-river."

This time it wasn't just Ed ready to throw a fit. How come I got put behind, too, when I was having such a good time up there on the bow, pushing the sail whichever way I was told and standing tall for the Klondike, just like sailors in some of them old stories? How come?

"Because there's a chance, maybe even a good chance, that we'll capsize and lose everything, and I'd rather be worrying about sacks of grub than my children, that's why, Billy."

"But, Pa," Ed said.

"Not another word, Sister. This is the way it's going to be."

That was a big blow for her and me, you can bet, but when Pa had that look, it wasn't no use to argue, and Ed knew it.

Jack didn't look our way, only whistled low while he hauled gear and grub out of the scow and put 'em on the sledge.

Ed slammed stuff this way and that, taking out her anger on sacks of flour and beans, like usual. But she didn't do no more than mutter until we were hauling the sledge, the two of us in harness.

"Billy, tell me, how come Pa believes everything Jack Purdy says?"

"I don't notice that he does."

"Sure he does. Jack Purdy says turn the boat this way, steer that way, haul down the sail now, and Pa just up and does it, like Jack Purdy is the boss instead of him."

Instead of *you,* I was thinking, but too smart to say so. After a while I said, "Well, anyhow, here we are, on the gold rush trail again, just you and me, like at Dyea."

"And suppose it ends up just you and me, with Pa drowned? I don't believe Jack Purdy knows as much as he boasts about boats or anything else. He just seen a good thing, throwing in with us, and worked his way into Pa's confidence. Like I don't have good judgment, when I'm the one got us out of Skagway and over Chilkoot."

I couldn't let that go by. "Be fair, Ed. We'd still be up there jawing with the Mounties if it wasn't for Jack."

She stopped for a moment and turned on me. "Oh, yes, you think he's all right. But, as Ma used to say, you ain't bothered with good judgment half the time."

"She never said that."

"Sure she did."

"You're a liar, Edna Rose," I said, and saw her eyes narrow at my charge.

"Well, maybe not in just those words, but that's what she meant, seeing how dreamy you were all the time and fearing you'd come to no good."

You can't argue with someone telling you what some other person thought, 'specially if that person can't talk for herself, so I just said, "Huh," and saved my breath for hauling the sledge over the rocky trail.

After we'd gone quite a distance, you could hear the faint roar of the Yukon down below.

"Ed?"

"What?"

"You recall the day Ma died, how she lay on the cot watching us?"

My sister bent lower, like she had to tug more on the sledge straps. "No, I don't."

"Her eyes followed us around, like she wanted to say something."

Ed trudged on, and it seemed a long while before she spoke again. "Well, she didn't, not to me, anyhow. Besides, I don't want to think about that, and you shouldn't, neither. You'd better be thinking about what we're going to do if Pa is drowned dead with all our goods."

"Jack Purdy won't let the boat capsize."

"Ha. I wouldn't put it past him to save himself and let Pa go. He's so shifty-eyed, a preacher wouldn't likely trust him to come up front and be saved."

"You don't let go of a thing very easy, Ed. Remember, Ma used to say you tended to cut off your nose to spite your face."

"Ma is gone," she said after a while. "It don't matter what she said."

Can you beat the way she would switch sides like that? One minute it was what Ma said about me was bound to be true. The next minute it was never mind what Ma said about her. I couldn't keep up with it. I thought of Ma, lying quiet in that unmarked grave back in Skagway, and wished she was here to set things straight.

By then we was coming down toward the river. You could see it through the trees, glistening and rolling on. I half expected to see Mounties waiting for us with bad news. Instead, it was Pa and Jack Purdy sitting on the bank, taking their ease in the afternoon sunshine.

My sister stopped for a moment, letting the sledge bump against her legs. "I declare," she whispered, and then commenced to shout, "Pa, Pa, here we are!"

"It was quite a ride," Pa said when we came closer. "We spun around at the edge of a whirlpool, and I thought sure the boat would swamp, but Jack kept cool and hung on that steering board like grim death. After that we come along at a pretty good clip. How was your hike?"

"Fine," Ed said, "just fine."

From then on she seemed to tolerate Jack being with us, although I never heard her speaking direct to him. If he was on the steering board, which he usually was, she might say, "Looks like we need to keep right, Pa." But she said it loud enough for Jack to hear. And when she rousted us out in the morning, she'd yell at nobody in particular, "As long as I'm up, everybody up!" Then, often as not, she'd kick my blanket roll.

Sometimes she rousted us out when it seemed like the middle of the night, so we could have our hasty breakfast and get going at first light. Every day we saw the ice creeping further out from the shore and clouds gathering earlier in the afternoons. Seemed like winter was coming south to meet us faster than we could go north.

When we had sailed across Lake LaBarge, Ed made dried-apple cobbler in celebration. Pa kept his word about not turning back after that point, but he said it was a mighty dangerous trek we was on and going to get worse, make no mistake.

There came a morning, it must've been two, three weeks after we launched at Lake Bennett, when Ed yelled louder than usual. She had the lantern lit and held it up to the side of our scow so we could see for ourselves how we was frozen fast to the shoreline. Except for a narrow channel in the middle, the Yukon River had gone still.

"Freeze-up," she said bitterly, like it was a trick being played on us.

"Well," Pa said. "We couldn't outrun Old Man Winter, after all."

10

ON FOOT TO THE KLONDIKE

WE TOOK THE SHEET STOVE and all the gear ashore, built a fire, and had our coffee and flapjacks in peace for once, and in daylight, too, but there wasn't much celebration. Pa gave orders to break up the scow, and we all set to, ripping the planks apart and turning them into a sled with Jack's metal strips fastened to the bottom for runners. It was hard, working fixed in one spot and trying not to think about your frozen feet and nose and forcing your fingers to keep moving inside mittens and gloves. But we kept at it until we had one big sturdy sled for the provisions and the small sledge for leftovers.

Then we began a slow trudge along the riverbank, always keeping it in sight so as not to lose our way. Sometimes we could travel on the river itself, if there was a fairly smooth stretch of ice, but mostly it froze in rough blocks that was heaved up and tilted at one another like they was in some kind of war. Then we had to break a trail alongside.

It was slow, lonely, and cold—so cold in the mornings, it made your lungs ache with the first breath you took outside the tent. We layered up our clothes over the suits of heavy underwear Pa picked up for us back at Lake Bennett, and covered up our faces as best we could. Pa said there must be others who had got caught by Old Man Winter same as us, but we didn't see them, nor any sign of winter camps.

After a few days of trudging, Ed began to limp when she thought no one was looking, but I saw. I mentioned it to Pa while he was fixing supper, after we had got the tent set up. He stopped filling a pot with beans and marched right over to Ed, who was huddled by the fire.

"Billy thinks your feet are giving you trouble, Sister. Is that true?"

Ed was surprised, but she covered fast. "Billy hardly ever knows what he's talking about. I turned my ankle a little, that's all, Pa."

"You're not getting chilblains or a touch of frostbite, are you, Miz McGee?" Jack asked.

Ed gave him a flinty look. "I know all about them ailments," she said, which was a flaming lie. We none of us knew a thing about traveling in such cold weather. Only Jack, who had lived through hard winters in Wisconsin, knew more. He said she should rub her feet good and wear more socks. He rummaged through his gear and got out a pair for her to borrow.

"These are extra. I'd appreciate you taking them."

"No thank you," she said.

"I don't aim to see you lose your toes for pride, Sister," Pa said. "You take off your boots and let me rub your feet, and then you put on them socks and tell Jack Purdy much obliged."

Her face went red, but she did like she was told. When she kicked me good and hard the next morning on wake-up call, I knew it was payment for tattling. I thought for once I had bested her, because I wasn't having trouble with my feet.

Maybe it was that notion made me kind of cocky and led to the accident a couple days afterward. What happened was this. Jack and me was hauling the big sled along the bank when I spied a smooth stretch of ice.

"Hey, Jack," I said, "looky there. We can go on the river a ways." I turned sharp and hit a slope I hadn't noticed. My feet went out from under me and I slid and then sprawled sideways down the bank, with the sled coming right along after me. Jack jerked so hard on his rope that the sled skewed around. I don't know how it happened exactly, but the end of a runner stabbed me hard in the ankle. I lay there sprawled out while Jack got the sled halted and came around to help.

"Whoa," he said, looking down at my leg. I didn't feel much of anything until he and Pa hauled me onto the sled and took off my boot. There was a fair-size gash, with blood oozing out. It began to throb after Pa cleaned it and fashioned a bandage. Although the day was only half gone, he said we should make camp. That meant losing time, I knew, and it didn't make me feel any better to see Ed stomping around like her feet was made of cast iron.

The next morning when she called breakfast, I crawled out of the tent, took one step, and fell over from the pain.

"I'll be right as rain after I eat," I said, remembering that I had fallen asleep before the beans got heated the night before.

When I'd finished off the flapjacks and hot tea, I tried to walk again, but couldn't seem to put any weight on that foot. I crawled back into the blankets while the others stood around holding their steaming tin cups and peering in at me through the tent flap.

"We could stay here until Billy gets better," Pa said, "though it ain't much of a camping place. Maybe we'd ought to turn back to Fort Selkirk."

"Turn back?" Ed said. "Oh, please, Pa, no."

"Well, what are we to do? The boy can't walk. And if that wound were to get infected . . ." He trailed off with a worried look on his face that got me to thinking that losing time might be the least of my concerns.

"You cleaned it out real good, Pa. I'll haul him on the little sled while you and Jack pull the big one."

"I don't know, Sister. Seems like too much. What do you think, Jack?"

Jack took a swallow of his tea and wiped his mouth.

"Miz McGee might be able to do it. Let's give it a try."

Right away Ed set to making a place for me amongst the softest provisions, the bags of flour and cornmeal. Then she covered me up with nearly all our blankets and said my main job was to heal up and not talk. We started again, going slower, of course. Jack and Pa, each with a rope around his chest, trudged ahead with the big sled, carrying near all our goods in a great pile with nobody behind to keep it going right. Ed would holler if it seemed likely to tip over, but mostly everyone saved their breath for the effort of walking.

I lay between the blankets and sacks feeling shamed and sorry for the fool thing I done, wondering whether my ankle would quit hurting after it froze solid and if there was a chance I might actually lose my foot. We'd had some fall of snow by then, and because of that the air wasn't as cold as it might've been. But for a person lying still, it was pretty cold.

After a while of watching mist and fog come off the frozen river and sift through the trees, I fell into a sort of daydream, thinking how dark and secret the country was. I recalled stories I'd heard of folks who froze to death. At first they ached with cold just like I did, but after a while they felt warm, even cozy. Then they went to sleep and never woke up. I wondered if that would happen to us. Or maybe to some of us, and the others would go right on walking to Dawson, which in my dream was a big town climbing over a hillside, with cabins all lighted and smoke coming out of chimneys.

Seemed like I could see into one cabin, where a woman was reading with the lamplight shining on her brown hair. It was Ma. She turned away from her book and looked out toward me, like she was going to say something. Then the lamp blinked out and the cabin seemed to melt into darkness, only I could still see the shape of it in a grove of trees. I squeezed my eyes shut, and when I opened them, the cabin was still there and we was going right by.

"Hey," I said in a croaky voice I hardly knew. "Hey, Ed."

My sister kept on trudging, so I croaked louder, "Ed, stop!"

She pulled the sledge sideways to anchor it against the snow and straightened up with her mittened hands on her back. "What's the matter, Billy, for pity's sake?"

"Looky there," I said, struggling to sit upright and point. "A cabin, ain't it?"

"What cabin?" Then she dropped her harness ropes and pitched forward, hollering, "Pa! Pa, come back!"

Pretty soon there came him and Jack, stumbling along, probably thinking something bad had happened.

"Look!" Ed said.

At first they couldn't believe it. "A cabin," Pa said in wonderment. "The very thing I was hoping and praying for since Billy's accident, and here it is."

"Let's go see," Jack said, and he and Pa went off through the untracked snow, saying me and Ed had to stay where we was. We watched them disappear in the little grove of trees. In the stillness you could hear the creak of a door opening, but there wasn't no welcoming voice. We waited what seemed a lengthy time, feeling the night cold coming down mean and hard.

"What are they doing, Ed?"

"I don't know, but it seems like something ain't right."

Finally, Pa and Jack came back.

"Can we stay, Pa? Is there a stove?"

"Yes," Pa said in a low voice. "There's a stove and some wood already cut and stacked. The old fella in there—owner or not, I don't know—won't be needing his firewood."

Not need a fire in the aching cold? "Why not, Pa?"

"Hush," Ed said, jerking the sledge rope so hard I nearly fell off. "Because he's dead, that's why. Ain't that right, Pa?"

He nodded.

"Maybe he was ailing when he got here, and then died of the cold," Jack said. "Looks like an old man, all alone."

For a moment the four of us stared at the silent cabin.

Then Pa said, "It seems to me, we should make a fire, get ourselves warm, and look to Billy's ankle. But first, Jack, you and me will get the sledge and take care of things inside."

That meant putting the old fellow somewhere, I

supposed. I never really got a look at him, but at first it made me feel funny to eat supper, bacon with beans, hot and tasty as it was, with him nearby. Then I got used to the notion and ate until I was full, and slept pretty well, too, after Pa had me soak my foot and ankle in warm salt water.

The next morning everyone except me searched through the old man's possessions: sacks of flour and beans, tools and blankets—almost as much as we had—and a supply of frozen fish, which we didn't have. They looked for some sign of who he was, where he came from, if he had partners or family, and found nothing except scribbles in a battered notebook. It didn't have any particular information according to Pa, beyond dates and the weather and a word or two on animals he saw.

"Let me see," I said, thinking I might decipher the writing. As soon as I stepped out, my leg gave way and I half fell against the table.

"Tarnation," I said as Pa hauled me upright and sat me on a stool. "Looks like I'm crippled."

"Stop whining," Ed said real brisk. "You're going to be fine."

"Miz McGee is right," Jack said. "You'll be dancing a jig before you know it." And he took a little turn around the cabin, his feet kicking out sideways, so comical I had to laugh.

Pa frowned and cut his eyes sideways, I guessed to let Jack know it wasn't seemly to be doing a jig with the old man just outside the door, behind the stacked-up stove wood.

"Beg pardon," Jack said, and sat himself down with another cup of coffee.

"I've been thinking," Pa said, "we might stay here a couple days to give Billy's ankle time to heal, and we can give the old man a decent burial, too."

"Good idea," Jack said. "What do you think, Miz McGee?"

Ed looked a little flustered. Up to then she hadn't been talking to Jack direct. "I guess that would be only right," she said finally, "since we're going to use his goods."

"Ah," Pa said, stroking his mustache. "That don't seem quite honest, to just be taking someone else's outfit."

"But, Pa, he don't need it and we do."

"She's right, Mr. McGee," Jack said.

Pa looked from one to the other. "I suppose we don't have much choice. Well, let that go for now, and let's us three scout for a good burial spot. Maybe we can find a place where the ground ain't froze clear through."

After they left, I crawled back to my blanket roll and slept some more. When I woke, I didn't recall where I was for a moment, all alone in the wilderness. Well, not entirely alone. The old man was close by. I fell to thinking about him and his life and wondering what his story might be. My foot throbbed something awful, but I did my best to ignore it. After a while I crawled over to the table where Pa had laid the notebook. There was hardly anything in it except scribbled notes that looked near impossible to decipher. But since I didn't have nothing to do, I got myself on a stump stool, propped up my leg, and went through the last part of the notebook as best I could.

Two or three entries before the end, something caught my eye. "Couldn't this morning . . ." There was a gap with words too blurry to read and then, "have to fend for themselves."

I rubbed at my gimpy leg and stared at the notebook page. What was that likely to mean? Who would have to fend for what? Couldn't be other people. Mules, maybe? Or dogs? Of course, dogs! That would explain the chunks of frozen fish . . . dogs . . . a dog team! Oh, glory, wouldn't that be something? I hopped over to the door, wincing against the pain, and looked out into the wilderness of trees and down toward the frozen river.

"Halloo, dogs, where are you?"

Everything was silent and still. No dark shapes came out of the bushes, but I couldn't shake the feeling that I was right. I hopped back to the stove, loaded in some more logs, and waited for Pa and the others to come back and hear my idea.

"Yes," Jack said later, "it makes sense. I saw footprints behind the cabin, not big enough for wolves."

"Hmm," Pa said. "Might be they left the old man

several days back when he quit feeding them. Probably they're well on their way to Dawson by now, or gone into the wild. I doubt they'll come back."

"Let's put out some of that frozen fish and see, Pa."

Pa put out fish the next morning and took it in untouched that evening. He did the same thing the morning that followed. That was the day we buried the old man. I was quite a bit better and limped to the burial on my own, Pa looking relieved that I seemed to be healing up right. We all stood around solemn while Pa read something from his Bible and smoothed dirt over the mound. Jack had dragged up a sizable river rock to mark the place, and I thought to myself, *We could've done that for Ma.* Too late now. Then we came back through the trees, still kind of solemn and silent. Ed was in the lead, and just as she reached the clearing, she stopped us all with her arm flung up. There was a critter hunched over the frozen fish. It lifted its head and backed off snarling, a shepherd sort of dog with dirty yellow fur and a white ruff around its neck and chest.

"Hullo, dog," I said, careful not to move sudden. The dog cocked its ears at me and went back to eating.

"Ain't that something?" Jack said. "I wonder where the others are."

"What others?" Ed asked. Right then, like they had heard, a couple more dogs came slinking out of the bushes. By and by more arrived, until there was six.

"A team," Pa said. "Get some more of that fish, Jack, if you will."

We all stood watching in wonderment while the dogs snapped and snarled over their dinner, taking care to keep out of the way of the one with the white ruff.

"Is that the lead dog, Pa?"

"Could be, son," he said, rubbing his mustache with his mittened hand.

"Well, then," Ed said, "we might have some help getting our outfits to Dawson, praise be."

"We'd be doing them a favor," Jack said. "Looks like these critters are having a hard time trying to make it on their own. And sled dogs are bred to run."

"I suppose since we're aiming to borrow a good deal of the old man's goods, it won't make our debt much worse to use his dog team," Pa said slowly, as if he were working things out in his mind.

"That's certain, and I don't need to tell you we need the help, Mr. McGee."

Pa went on rubbing his mustache. "Well," he said, "this is a rougher trek than even I reckoned, but I hate to just take things that ain't mine."

"Pa, he can't use this stuff anymore."

"That's true, Sister, but still . . ."

"Maybe someone in Dawson will know about the old man, and we can square it then," Jack said.

Pa looked up, almost grateful. "Good idea, Jack. I'll write a list of what we're making off with." He moved toward the cabin carefully, so as not to scare away the dogs. "Where's that notebook?"

Ed said she was going to look for the dog-team harnesses, and Jack said he would help her. They walked off together, leaving me thinking about how nice it would be not to have to pull the sled and how glad I was for the old man's cabin.

Ed and Jack found the harnesses and other lines back in the woods behind the cabin, stashed under a tarpaulin, which also covered a dog sled. They decided we could haul the sled we'd made and have the dogs haul the one they was used to. Turned out, with what the old man had left, grub and tools and blankets and the like, there was too much to haul even with two sleds. Pa said we should cache some stuff and come back for it later.

While they were fussing with goods, sorting and packing, I saw to the dogs, chopping the frozen fish and parceling it out. That night the dogs disappeared into the bushes, but the next morning they was there again, yapping for their food. The lead dog, the yellow one with the white chest and collar, always got first dibs, and then the others could eat. She was female, which I guessed was unusual for a lead, but you wouldn't want to tangle with her over that. If the others came too close while she was getting her feed, she snapped at them, and they backed off respectful. I was kind of wary of her, too, but she seemed to take to me well enough. None of the dogs had names that we knew, of course, so we were free to call them any old thing. I named them all for people in the storybook that Tom Thunder had took back in Smuggler's Cove: Ajax, Cyclops, Hector, Neptune, and Jason. The lead dog, I decided, would be Persephone, after a girl who went into the underworld and, when she came back each year, brought spring with her.

Ed laughed. "People call sled dogs things like King and Jocko, or maybe Queenie," she said. "They don't name 'em after characters in Greek tales."

"*I* do," I said. "Her name's Persephone, and I'll call her Persey for short. I believe me and her will be friends."

"Don't get too attached, Billy. They're only work dogs, you know."

That seemed a dumb thing to say, since we was depending on them to get us to Dawson and might not make it without, which she herself knew. But I didn't argue.

When the supplies were divvied up and the sleds loaded with as much as they could bear, and the rest of the stuff hid away, we were ready to start. Pa insisted on leaving a stack of stove wood and a small bag of beans for anybody else who might come along desperate the way we had been. Then he and Jack straightened out the harnesses and put them on the dogs.

A strange thing happened as soon as the dogs were in harness. They fell into place, with Persey and Ajax in the lead, and when they were fastened to the gang line, they begun to jiggle and strain to move. Jack was right. Those dogs wanted to run. They took off yipping, almost happy, it seemed, and us, too. My ankle was still sore to the touch but had pretty well healed, and I felt good running alongside the team and talking at Persey. Pretty soon we crossed the mouth of the Stewart River, where there was supposed to be a trading post, but we didn't stop to look.

Sometimes we spied traces of other folks who had gone before us, but we never saw a soul. It was just us and our dog team mushing northward to the gold fields, going along at such a good pace that even Ed came close to being cheerful.

11

DAWSON, CITY OF GOLD

I BEGAN TO DAYDREAM about Dawson the last few days of travel, seeing in my mind's eye a grand city like Seattle. When we came around a last bluff over the frozen river and saw the huddle of gray buildings with smoke drifting over them like fog, I was a little set back.

We crossed over the mouth of the Klondike River and went on through a pitiful settlement that was mostly tents or small huts laid out higgledy-piggledy. Later we learned that part was called Louse Town, which gives you an idea what folks thought of it.

Dawson itself wasn't a whole lot better, being mostly a row or two of buildings built back a little ways from the river. In between the shore and town was a roadway of frozen muck. Some buildings were made of logs, and others was framed up with sawn planks. Most of those had high square fronts that made them look big, but the front part didn't match the back. There were clusters of cabins, some made from boat parts that you could still see, like ghosts of what they used to be.

Besides thinking it might be a real city, I had figured Dawson would be a place where people danced in the streets, swinging their bags of gold. There were people in the streets, all right, but they was all bundled up against the terrible cold and they trotted out of one place and into another as fast as they could. If they had gold, it didn't show.

We made our way along the road, inquiring about lodging. Folks pointed out cabins we could have for the taking, leastwise for a while, as their owners had left before freeze-up. We chose one that seemed built sturdy enough and unloaded the sleds. Lucky we had our sheet-iron stove, because someone had already scavenged what was in the cabin. After we got everything inside, Pa said his next job was to make inquiry about the old man back at Stewart River and me and Persey could go with him.

We trudged from one end of Dawson to the other, going in and out of every establishment where the door wasn't locked. Each store and saloon had a set of brass balance scales sitting out where everyone could see. According to Pa, that was for weighing the gold dust that people used instead of money. I figured it might be a good job to wipe the counters and sweep the floors in those places. Pa said the storekeepers already knew to look for that kind of dust.

A lot of places were saloons filled up pretty solid with men sitting around. People was glad to jaw with us because it seemed not much was going on in town. The big claims, they told us, was some miles southeast, along the Klondike and its pup creeks, the Eldorado and the Bonanza. Out there prospectors was digging in the frozen earth even now, in the half dark of winter, looking for gold, while some people in town already had theirs and nowhere much to spend it. Nearly everyone was worried their food supplies wouldn't hold out until spring. The last ships bringing supplies upriver from St. Michael, hundreds of miles west, had froze in about halfway, and nobody expected other steamers to try. People were interested to hear how we had come from Lake Bennett and said we was lucky to have made it.

That made a good opening for Pa's query about the old man at Stewart River. Soon as he started in on that, somebody would chime in with his own tale of men who got separated from their partners one way or another and couldn't find each other ever again, and of other folks who died nameless and alone.

"I tell you, stranger," one old-timer said, hooking his thumbs into his suspenders and leaning back against the bar, "there's plenty men in the Yukon Valley that would just as soon nobody knew where they had gone and wouldn't carry nothing that would tell. Maybe the sheriff is after them back home, or they got debts they couldn't pay or a family they couldn't support. Better to leave sleeping dogs lie, if you know what I mean." He nodded and gave his suspenders a snap. "Speaking of dogs, that's a good one you got there, sonny. Pity it isn't part of a team."

"She is," I said proudly, "and she's a real good lead dog, too."

"Well," said the old-timer, "a good team would probably fetch a high price these days from somebody hoping to get out of here."

"She ain't for sale," I said.

Pa gave me a sideways look, I thought maybe to warn me off from saying the team didn't really belong to us.

We had the conversation about the old fella at Stewart River several times and always with the same result, but Pa kept at it, until a storekeeper told him to go down the street to the Territory Commissioner's office.

The Canadian officer there knew about the cabin. He said it was used by whoever needed it and didn't belong to anyone in particular. Furthermore, he had no record of a man such as Pa described being among the missing. "That's not unusual," he said in his high-class voice. "Many of your compatriots seem to be anonymous or to have names that can't be traced." He made note of Pa's description of the old man and said it would be kept on file. Then he thanked Pa for his honesty.

"Not at all," Pa said. "My family and my partner owe that old fella a debt."

"To be sure. His bad fortune was your good one," the officer said as he closed his book.

We made our way back toward our cabin in the early dark with Persey leading us. What Pa said about his "partner" stuck in my thoughts.

"Will Jack move on now, Pa?"

"Huh?" he said. "What are you talking about, Billy?"

"What you were saying to the officer about your partner. Edna Rose made you promise Jack was to be partners just until we got to Dawson."

"Well, now, son, that's another question we need to answer, I guess."

We got back to the place and found that Ed and Jack had stowed things away pretty well. They had the other dogs tied up in a shed in back and supper on the stove.

"Any luck?" Jack wanted to know.

Pa shook his head. "No one claims to know a thing about him, although maybe they would if we said how much stuff he left behind."

"I trust you didn't," Ed said.

"No, I didn't," Pa replied, "and that don't make me rest easy, either. I'm trying to figure what's fair."

"Fair?" she said, bursting out so suddenly we all looked at her in surprise. "Was it fair the lumber mill closed and you didn't have work and we lived on oatmeal mush? Was it fair for Ma to get sick without warning and then just die without another word? I don't think fair has got anything to do with anything in this country."

Pa stroked his mustache and studied her, maybe trying to figure out how come she had got so tough. "I know you've had a hard time, Sister—I know that," he said, and I near choked on my tea. *How come Ed don't get yelled at for talking back?* I wanted to ask.

Pa went on. "But I ain't going to give up all my principles just because of hard times. So I'll keep the list I made in the old man's notebook, and if anyone turns up claiming his goods, we can figure out a settlement."

"Then we'd better get to prospecting," Ed said, "and plan to hit pay dirt." She had heard that talk somewhere and was already carrying on like she knew something about hunting for gold.

"That brings up another question," Pa said. "Are we all in this prospecting business together?"

I held my breath, wondering what we'd do without Jack. Maybe the others was wondering the same thing. Nobody was looking at anybody, just down at their hands or knees or at whatever they was pretending to be doing.

"I'm willing to throw in my lot with you McGees," Jack said after a while, "but if that ain't agreeable, I'll go my way."

"Ah, no, Jack, don't go," I said.

"That's my thought, too," Pa added.

Then we was all waiting for my sister, Ed. She turned her back and went to stirring what was in the pot for supper—cornmeal mush, from the smell of it. "If he comes in as partners, how are we going to divvy things? Like who's got the say about what we do? Would his vote be equal to yours, Pa, or to mine?" You could see her mind was still roiling with who got to be boss.

Pa said he hoped for general agreement, and since we'd shared the old man's goods, he figured we'd share anything else.

"That don't seem quite right," Ed said. She began to spoon out the mush with some salt pork to the side. "Since there are three of us and one of him."

"Well," Jack began after a long wait while we listened to the soft plop of mush landing on our plates, "how about two thirds for McGees and one third for Purdy?"

Any fool with a couple years of arithmetic would see that only worked if one of us McGees didn't count for a full share—that being me, most likely. But I didn't speak up, for the reason I wanted Jack to stay with us.

"If you're willing to accept that, I am," Pa said. "Sister, how about you?"

Ed put the pot back on the stove. She was all red from the heat, even sweating a little, though it was cold as anything outside. "Yes," she said finally, swiping her forehead where the hair lay plastered down. "That's all right by me. Billy, you'd better put that dog out with the others and feed her. This hothouse ain't no place for a sled dog."

I was kind of disappointed that it was settled so easy and we didn't get to watch Ed go into a rant, but mostly I was glad. Maybe, I thought, my sister was losing some of the meanness she took on when Ma died and would be back to her old self soon.

By the time I got back from feeding Persey and making sure she was locked in with the rest of the team, they was talking about how Jack and me should take the sled and dog team back to Stewart River for the goods we'd left, while Ed and Pa would scout around for the best place for us to live. Ed was all for going to Grand Forks, at the junction of the Bonanza and Eldorado, where we'd heard some rich strikes had been made and where there was already a little settlement.

"No point in traipsing back and forth from Dawson," she said, "if we can find a place out there and start digging right outside the door."

She and Pa set off on foot to find that place the same morning that Jack and I went back upriver. With so little to haul, seemed like we fairly flew over the trail. I rode sometimes, and Jack rode other times. When it was downhill, we both rode, whooping and hollering and enjoying ourselves. We got to the Stewart River in jig time.

The cabin was just as we left it—no sign of other travelers having been there, and nothing disturbed at the cache, either. After we loaded the sled, I roamed off with Persey while Jack went hunting. Persey was a sled dog all right and took that life serious, but she had learned to unbend a little with me. She accepted my petting her and maybe even liked it, while the other dogs seemed to want only their fish and the harness and running. That afternoon Persey and me rolled around in the snow and sneaked through the woods, pretending we was looking for snow rabbits, which Jack actually was, for our supper.

He came back in the early twilight, with a rabbit dangling by his side, and stood watching me roughhouse with Persey. "I hope you aren't getting too friendly with that dog," he said.

"Why not?"

"We might not be able to feed the dogs this winter, Billy. Likely we'll have trouble feeding ourselves."

"Sure we can, Jack. If they're not running, they won't need much food."

He gave me a long look with his head cocked in that way he had, so you didn't know whether to take him serious or not. Then he went into the cabin.

We had rabbit stew for supper with a potato and some carrots from our cache, and it was mighty tasty. I ate my fill for once and settled back for a nice evening of sitting by the stove, my arm around Persey's neck, while Jack and me traded stories like we did coming down from Chilkoot.

"Tell me some more of them troll stories, Jack, that your grandma told you."

He had taken up a piece of stove wood and was starting to carve it. "I don't have a grandma, Billy—not that I know about, anyway."

"But you said you did."

"Calling an old woman grandma is just a way of speaking. She was the cook in the county home, and from the color of my hair she thought maybe my folks had come from Finland, same as her. But she wasn't kin to me." I watched the shavings curl and fall away from his carving. "Truth to tell, I don't really have any folks," he said after a while.

"What about the sister you thought Edna Rose was when you came back from near drowning?"

"I did have a sister a long time ago, older than me. After our folks died, she hired out and I was sent to the county home." He raised up and threw his carving into the fire. "I heard she got married, but whoever told me that had lost track of what name she went by. For a while I looked for her, then gave it up and came west on my own."

I was thinking how it would be if I'd lost both Pa and my sister after Ma was gone. "Ah, Jack," I said, "it's awful sad not to have folks of your own."

He got another piece of wood and began working on it. "Well," he said, "it is sad, Billy, but you get used to it." He worked fast, making shavings fall away from the chunk of wood, which he then held up and studied. "And then you get a surprise like I did, meeting up with you and your pa and Miz McGee."

I didn't know what to make of that and sat quiet for a time, working it over in my mind. The stove was burning pretty hot by then, and Persey wriggled away from me and went to whining at the door.

“Better let her out,” Jack said. “It’s too hot in here for a sled dog.”

I opened the door and watched Persey bound away across the snow. I was disappointed because I had kind of hoped she would sleep by my side that night. When I came back and sat down again, Jack patted my shoulder.

“I can see how much store you set by that dog. I expect it’ll be hard to let her go.”

“What are you talking about?” I said, suddenly stiff.

He held up his carving again and squinted at it this way and that. “If it comes to having to sell the team,” he said.

“We can’t do that, Jack. They ain’t ours to sell.”

“Whose are they, then?”

“You know as good as me, they belong to that old man, lying out there.”

“No, we don’t know that. All we know is they were abandoned here and we fed ’em and used ’em, and maybe we’ll have to pass ’em along to the next fella who needs a team.”

I stared at him open-mouthed. “You sound like my sister, Ed,” I said finally.

“She’s not always wrong, Billy.”

“Ha. That’s what you think. Anyway, Pa wouldn’t sell Persey. He knows she’s come to be my own dog.”

“Didn’t you just say the dogs really belonged to the old man?”

“Ha,” I said again, mad at being tripped up. Right then some of the warm feelings I had for Jack—how he was my friend before he was anyone else's, and how we was sort of in cahoots against my sister—some of that began to feel different.

He showed me what he had been working on—a little dog, it was. "It's for you when I finish. I'm sorry I made you feel bad."

"You didn't," I said, "because you don't know about our family. You ain't been around a family enough to know how they do things."

"Right," he said. And that was the end of our talking and of the evening I had been looking forward to, just Jack and me, telling our tales to each other. I pulled my book of pirate stories out of my pack and tried my best to concentrate on reading them until it was time to turn in for the night.

By the next morning I had myself believing that Jack truly didn't know anything about my pa. How could he, a stranger who didn't even know much about his own pa?

Neither of us mentioned the talk again, and as soon as we got going, running alongside the sled through the snowy woods and down along the frozen river, I begun to feel better. I was proud how I handled the team and dreamed I might go into the business of packing goods on my own one day. I might even make a fortune without having to dig for it. Wouldn't that put my sister's nose out of joint?

12

WINTER 1898

AFTER WE GOT BACK TO DAWSON, we began hauling stuff to where Ed and Pa had found another cabin. It was on the west side of Eldorado Creek, not far from the little settlement called Grand Forks, and only needed some inside work to make it good enough for the four of us. Most important, it was abandoned, so we wouldn't have to pay rent to anybody.

Still, it seemed like Pa was plenty worried about having enough cash to buy what we'd need. I watched him go through his old leather purse over and over and shake his head about the price of lumber.

"It ain't just the cabin," he said. "We'll have to have enough to buy some tools for mining."

Jack had given every cent he had, which wasn't much, and of course Ed and I didn't have a nickel to add.

One evening when I was sitting by the stove reading my book, I noticed that all the talking had stopped and the three of 'em was staring at me.

"I just been saying, it looks like we got to consider selling the dog team, Billy," Pa said.

I went back to my book.

"Did you hear me, son? It's more than just buying lumber—it's trying to feed six hungry dogs all winter. We just can't do it."

I looked from one to the other—Pa stroking his mustache like he always did when he was disturbed, Jack watching me with his head cocked, and my sister, Ed, who I figured was the ringleader, staring down at her hands.

"Well," I said as cool as I could, "it might be you'll have to sell the team—I don't know about that. But you can't sell Persey."

"Dog team's not much good without the lead dog," Pa said.

"I don't care," I said. "You can't have her."

"She's a sled dog, son. You don't want to keep her from doing the thing she's bred to do, the thing that makes her happy, do you?"

"Yes, I do! She's as much my dog as she is any of yours, since we stole the whole lot from that poor old dead man at Stewart River!"

Pa rose off his log stool. "What'd I hear you say, son?"

For an answer I jumped up, grabbed my parka and mittens, and ducked out, then went to the shed to get

Persey. Soon her and me was going along Front Street as fast as we could in the frigid air.

It was close to dark on a Sunday evening, and lots of places were closed by Canadian law. Some people was holding a church service in the assayer's shop. I could hear them singing the evening hymn, and that brought Ma to my mind. She could carry a tune better than most and used to sing that same hymn on Sundays. Me and Persey kept walking and the tune floated along behind us. Would Ma want me to give up my dog? *Well, maybe, if you can't feed her,* came an answer in my head.

Persey trotted on, happy to be on the move, even in air so cold it made your lungs hurt. Finally, I couldn't keep it up and called her back. Then I buried my face in her thick ruff.

"Persey, don't you want to stay with me?"

She only whined and struggled to be free, to keep trotting over the frozen ground, or maybe to get back to the shed for her supper. I turned back, telling myself that whatever happened, I wasn't going to bawl and Ed wouldn't never have another chance to call me crybaby. Still, I was mighty close to it when I saw someone in the roadway walking crossways and back and beating mittened hands against his arms. It was Pa.

I came up to him, and we stood a moment looking at each other.

"Son, I'm going to let it go how you talked just now, because I see how much that dog means to you. And another thing I see is how tough you are. Look at all you done. You took care of your ma as best you could, you saved a man's life, you climbed Chilkoot Pass, helped build a boat, and came down the Yukon on the edge of winter."

I didn't say anything.

"That shows you can do pretty near anything when you have to—like giving up your dog for the sake of the family."

"Pa, we only come to have the team because that old man froze to death, and now you and them are acting like having dogs to sell was part of our plan all along."

"What you say is God's truth, and I feel bad about it," Pa said, all the time kind of working me around so we was headed back to the cabin. "Still, I got to figure out how we can survive winter in this country, let alone prospect for gold. If we get lucky like your sister thinks we will, I'll buy your dog back or get you another one. I swear I will, Billy."

He looked at me so grieved, and with frost on his mustache and eyebrows, that I couldn't speak.

"I'm asking you to be a man about this, son."

It came to me that folks always talk about you being grown-up when they want you to do something you don't want to do.

"Okay," I said finally. "But I won't forget." Then I took Persey to the shed and held her tight for a moment, like she was about to go right then.

Jack and Ed was sitting together at the plank table.

They both looked up, like people do when they've just been talking about you but pretend they haven't.

"Pretty cold out tonight," Jack said.

"Want some hot tea?" Ed asked.

I didn't give them the satisfaction of an answer, but went back to reading my book and didn't look up even when Ed came over and brushed her hand across my head. I figured she knew I'd given in and was trying to hide how good she felt about being right again. Jack, too, probably.

Nothing happened until we had finished hauling all the lumber and gear to the new place. Then, one morning, Jack got up early and put the dogs in harness.

"Maybe you want to say goodbye to Persey," he said when he had 'em all jiggling and ready to go.

"I done that," I replied, "no thanks to you."

He cocked his head, looking at me through his slanty eyes, then went off running alongside the team, Persey trotting fit to bust like always.

He came back toward evening, on foot and carrying Pa's old purse full of coins, with some nuggets and gold dust, too.

"Folks bid up the price pretty good," he said, spilling it out. "The ones that don't have enough grub on hand are looking to mush out any way they can." He turned toward me. "Billy, the man that won the bidding says Persey is a fine dog and he'll take good care of her."

I turned away without answering.

In fact, after that I generally stopped talking to the whole crowd, unless I had to. I figured since I was a no-vote member of the partnership, I didn't have to pass the time of day with 'em. They tried, of course, even Ed, but mostly we was all busy getting the place ready, working quick since the days was so short.

Pa was a good carpenter, and it turned out Jack was, too. They took time to cut out two windows and cover them tight with canvas. You couldn't see out, but some light came in. They built a lean-to where we could store tools and grub and have more room inside. Ed said she wanted a sleeping loft for herself, being the only female, and, of course, they done that. Then Jack and Pa made another loft on the other side and said it was for me. If they'd asked, I would've said, *No, I don't want nothing special from you,* but since it was a done thing, I hauled my stuff up there quick enough.

As soon as we'd quit work for the day, I'd get close to the fire or lantern or whatever light there was and stick my nose in one of my books, hardly stopping long enough to eat supper. The pirate book was all right, but those stories thinned out after a while and I spent most of my time with the other book. It was about a boy named David Copperfield. He had more hard luck even than I did. His mother had died, too, but he had a stepfather who treated him mean and made him work in a bottle factory. I had read the story before, but it had more meaning for me now. So that's how I made it through those first days without Persey, and after a while, I got used to being lonely.

13

PA'S VOTE

OUR PLACE was on the west side of where Eldorado Creek joined the bigger one, the one that used to be called Rabbit Creek before gold was discovered and now was called Bonanza. Folks said it was the richest creek in the world. Grand Forks was at the junction, a little settlement with a few places for selling provisions and lumber, a laundry, and a couple sorry-looking log cabins with sod roofs that called themselves hotels. The best place was the Grand Forks Hotel. It had two stories, a porch in front, and sheds out back for storage and dog teams. It was owned and run by a woman named Miz Belinda Mulrooney. Everyone acted respectful toward her, too, especially since they saw what good business she was doing.

Just before the cabin got finished was my birthday, and Pa said we would have our dinner at Grand Forks Hotel to celebrate. I knew he was trying to make up to me on account of Persey. I wasn't going to give way on that, 'specially since I figured it was some of the coins from selling Persey that was paying for our dinner. But still, it was mighty nice to have a reason to wash my face and go somewhere else for eats. Miz Mulrooney didn't serve us, but she came out and said hello. She wore a long black skirt and a white shirtwaist, starched and clean like nothing I'd seen since we left Skagway.

"How's your prospecting going?" she asked.

"We're just about to start that, ma'am. You got any good pointers where we should dig?" Pa said.

Miz Mulrooney laughed like that was some kind of joke and went on to the next table to say hello there.

Of course, we was on our own for gold hunting, like everybody else. It turned out that my sister, for all her gumption and fire to get to the Klondike, didn't have no more idea where to look for gold than a hoot owl. That was all right, but what I held against her was the way she had made it sound like a grand adventure, instead of the miserable, cold, dirty business it was, tromping around in the winter fog and dusk, looking for a place to dig in the froze hard ground. You'd come across other people, kind of ghostlike in the mist, doing the same thing. Or, having found a likely place, groaning as they heaved their pickaxes to pry up a few inches of frozen muck and, when they got that done, building a fire to thaw out a few more inches. Winter in the Klondike meant short, bitter cold days and long, even colder nights, and after the few hours of daylight faded, you could see little fires flickering along the creek banks and know folks was still at it. The green wood sent up smoke that thickened the winter fog so much that sometimes you didn't know where you'd got to, except you guessed by the sound of axes cutting trees further up on the hills and the creak of windlasses as folks hauled up buckets of frozen dirt and dumped them in piles to be washed out when the streams ran again in spring.

All the way along the Bonanza and the Eldorado, places had been claimed every hundred square feet, or what folks thought was a hundred square feet, because that was the rule for a claim. When the government surveyor came through, he surveyed each claim all over again. If it was short, that was your hard luck. If it was too long, you had to let go of the extra for someone else to claim. People fought and schemed like anything over some of those leftover pieces of creek bank, called fractions. A couple of those turned out to be worth thousands, but most were worthless.

My sister got it fixed in her mind that one of the fractions was on top of a vein of gold. Pa and Jack was doubtful, but she talked them into digging a shaft. After lots of hard work thawing and digging, we didn't turn up more than maybe a sprinkling of gold dust when the dirt was panned out in the cabin. Still, Ed stuck to her guns, saying that fraction was bound to turn up pay dirt, seeing how close it was to a rich claim.

If we didn't stake it pretty quick, someone else would.

Pa finally gave in and went all the way to the government office at Forty Mile to stake the claim. One person–one claim was the rule, and you had to be over eighteen, so that meant we had only one more chance, which was for Jack to stake a claim, if this one didn't work out.

All through the worst part of winter, we built fires, thawed muck, dug it out, piled it up, and dug some more. Two of us would be in the hole with the lantern and two above, one to turn the windlass, hauling up buckets of dirt, and the other to dump them and send the bucket down again. We dug ten feet down and never hit bedrock or came up with a pail full of dirt that yielded more than the few flecks of gold we'd seen right at the beginning. Finally, even Ed had to admit there wasn't much reason to keep digging there.

It was pretty gloomy that night in the cabin. Jack tried to cheer us up by telling funny stories. Pa liked a good tale as much as anybody and told a couple himself. Still, Ed looked mighty down in the mouth. I thought it served her right, for being such a know-it-all and making us waste one of our two chances on a claim that was no good. I didn't know how we was ever going to buy a stone for Ma's grave and get back to Skagway if we didn't find a way to hit pay dirt.

Thinking about Ma just then put me in the mind that maybe I should be a little easier with my sister, despite her mean and stubborn ways. So I said, "Maybe you'd ought to tell one of your troll stories, Jack. Won't scare Ed. Might even cheer her up."

She gave me a look, and Jack laughed. "All right," he said. "This one is special for Miz McGee." He jumped into a wild tale about trolls making terrible trouble and giants who couldn't get rid of 'em and I don't know what all. It went on and on. Finally, he said, "There, now, Miz McGee, what do you think of that?"

"It'll do," she said—not what you'd call gracious but not outright rude, neither.

Well, for another couple weeks we roamed back and forth along the froze creeks, looking for a likely spot and not finding one. Prospectors was all around in the gulches and bottomlands doing what we was doing. Some of them had found gold. You knew that mostly by how they acted, like not wanting to talk much or pass the time of day, or you'd know it by the sneaky way they dumped their buckets of muck and covered them with a tarp.

About then came the morning when Ed went rooting through our pile of supplies in the lean-to shed, like she did from time to time. But that morning she set up a yell. "Where's that slab of bacon, Billy, and the other bag of cornmeal?"

I was stirring up dough for flapjacks, it being my turn to make breakfast. "Everything we got is right there."

"No, it ain't. I saw that bacon a little while back

and counted the sacks of cornmeal, too. One's missing."

I took the fry pan off the stove and went out and helped her search, but we didn't find either bacon or cornmeal. She knew, she said, she absolutely *knew* we had three more twenty-pound sacks of cornmeal, enough to keep us through the spring. Now one was gone, along with a big slab of bacon that was only a little moldy.

"Could be you miscounted in the first place," I said as we came back in from the lean-to.

"No such thing," she insisted. "They were from the old man's cache."

"Well, then, since we took 'em off him, maybe somebody took 'em off us."

"Oh, Billy, lay off that. This is serious."

"What's serious, Miz McGee?" asked Jack, coming in with a bucket of ice for making coffee water.

"We're missing grub—cornmeal and the last of the bacon."

Jack agreed that was serious and was for going through all our supplies again, but before we got started, there came Pa with a load of stove wood and he had to hear from Ed again what was missing.

"Ah," he said, looking kind of funny. "I took 'em."

Well, there was a space of silence, you can bet, while my sister struggled with herself and Jack and I stared at Pa.

"Last week, the day I was out hunting for rabbits, I came across a squaw and her children in a miserable little camp up on French Creek. They was starving to death, the five of 'em. Her man had gone off some time before to hunt food and never came back, maybe dead himself. I gave her the rabbit I had and then came on back here. But it kept nagging at me, how we had got that grub for nothing and maybe we were obliged to share it. So yesterday, without thinking much further, I took a bag of meal and a slab of bacon to her. And just in time, I reckon."

"Oh, Pa," Ed said, as close to tears as I'd seen her since we left Tacoma. "I cannot believe you'd do such a thing."

"We have enough to share," he said. "We ain't about to starve."

"That shows all *you* know," she said, with tears truly starting out of her eyes. "The flour's getting low, and the potatoes we need to keep from getting scurvy are almost rotten, and we may not have enough beans to last." Pa tried to pat her on the shoulder, but she jerked away. "You were the one said we all had to agree on things, Pa."

"I know, Sister, but you three were out of the cabin, and I was here alone when I was overcome by the notion that that woman and her young ones was going to be on my conscience forever if I didn't do something." He took off his mackinaw jacket, which you could hardly tell had ever been red. "I figure your ma would've done the same, so I counted her vote."

"And you could have mine, too . . . if I had a vote,"

I said. Why I came out with that, I don't know. I was as hungry as anybody else.

Ed sunk down on one of the stump stools, with her head in her hands. Jack shifted from one foot to the other, and I went back to making flapjacks, since we might as well have breakfast before we starved. I even got a few dried apples to stick in the batter and then boiled up the coffee. I laid out breakfast for myself and three sorry-looking people, just like I seen it done down at the Grand Forks Hotel, when a gold miner came in with a sad story. At that thought another one popped into my head.

"Come and get your grub," I said, "and listen to my idea."

Since they sold the team, I had mostly stayed out of the partner discussion business, so the three of them looked at me in some surprise. I made them wait while I hacked up my flapjack. "When I was down at Grand Forks the other day, I heard Miz Mulrooney speaking sharp to a fellow she'd hired to chop wood and sweep and serve in the dining room. She was telling him to pick up his wages and skedaddle. I'm thinking I could take his place."

"How's that going to help, if there isn't anything to buy?" Jack said.

"I heard that Miz Mulrooney laid by plenty of grub last fall. Maybe she'll trade work for a sack of cornmeal."

Ed looked at me, thoughtful. "You may have an idea, Billy."

"Well," said Pa, letting out his breath like he'd got off the hook, "I say you and Billy go down there tomorrow and see if you can strike a bargain."

Next morning, as soon as it was light, Ed and I got ourselves fixed up as best we could, washing in near freezing water and putting on clothes that was more or less clean but looked grimy, like everyone else's. Ed's hair had grown out considerable, only not straight like it used to be. She had these kind of loopy curls, and that day she brushed them something fierce. I was struck for a moment, seeing how different she looked from the Ed I had in my mind's eye, but I laid it to putting our best foot forward for Miz Mulrooney.

We walked along pretty brisk in the morning cold. The ground was chewed up below the hotel. Dirty snow and froze mud was tramped into slush some places, so we stepped careful. You wouldn't want to track any more dirt into Miz Mulrooney's place than you could help, particularly if you was coming to ask a favor.

Miz Mulrooney had a stern look and seemed old to me, although I guess she wasn't really. She wore her hair up and had eyeglasses pinched on her nose or hanging on a ribbon, and she always wore a pressed black skirt and a spanking white shirtwaist. How she kept things looking so clean was a mystery.

"What can I do for you?" she asked.

"Good morning," Ed said in a sweet voice I didn't

know she still had. "We heard you might be needing someone to chop wood and sweep. My brother is a good hand at that sort of work."

Miz Mulrooney put up her little oval spectacles and stared at me. "Billy McGee, is it?" she said. "You heard I might be looking for a young fellow, did you?"

I held back a little. It was, after all, eavesdropping that had got me that information. "Well, yes, ma'am," I said finally.

She looked at me closer through those spectacles. "Keep your ears open, do you?"

"Uh, yes, ma'am."

Probably Ed did not think that was likely to get me work chopping and sweeping. "He's real strong, Miz Mulrooney, and has been digging shafts and hauling buckets of frozen dirt along with the rest of us."

"I packed over Chilkoot, too," I said.

Miz Mulrooney let herself give a little smile. "So did I, young fellow. Well, now, people who work for me have to keep my rules and put in a day's work for a day's wage, which is two dollars."

"My brother wants to work in exchange for grub," Ed said. "Cornmeal and flour."

"There's more money than grub around here, as you know well enough. You folks having much luck with your prospecting?"

Ed looked her straight in the eye. "No, ma'am," she said. "Not much, but if we have enough grub to keep going, we'll be all right."

Miz Mulrooney knew we hadn't made a strike, like she knew just about everything that was going on around the creeks. But I didn't learn that until later, when I begun to see how sharp she listened to what prospectors were saying as they ate their dinners or sat by the fire smoking their pipes afterward. What she didn't hear direct, she expected people like me to report. Listening careful was almost as important to her as sweeping careful and keeping an eye out for spilled gold dust.

"Very well," she said. "I do have a little extra in the way of victuals I could spare for a good worker who keeps his ears open. You can start right now, Billy, if you like."

"Yes, ma'am," I said. "Whoopee!"

14

THE MAN IN THE RED CAP

SO THAT'S HOW I got my first real paying job, sweeping out the dining room and bar early in the morning when things was quiet and folks had gone upstairs to sleep. At first, that and chopping wood was mostly what I did, but soon Miz Mulrooney had me helping in the dining room and sweeping upstairs in the big dormitory room, with its two tiers of bunks running along each side and some curtains around for a little privacy. There was plenty of work to do, almost as heavy as digging in the frozen muck, but more various and with people to talk to—or rather to listen to, since no one was much interested in what a boy had to say.

Fairly regular, Miz Mulrooney called me into her little room where she kept the accounts. She'd figure my pay for however many days I'd worked that week and turn it into victuals to take back to the cabin. Then she'd ask me what was new, what talk I might've heard while prospectors were stretching out their legs after a meal, or what they mumbled about upstairs in the dormitory. She was game to hear any kind of gossip, but what interested her most was rumors of strikes, and who was staking what claim, and was he looking for a partner? From what folks said, Miz Mulrooney was already partners in half a dozen claims and seemed to be looking for more. I was pretty good at telling her everything, mostly keeping close to what people said, but sometimes I fixed things up just a little, to make 'em more interesting.

"You know, Billy McGee," she said one day, "you're pretty sharp at this business of reporting. You can make a good story out of not much, like any respectable newspaper fellow." She was looking at me through her little glasses.

"Well, ma'am," I said, "I aim to be truthful, mostly."

"I know, but you add a little color now and again. Don't tell me you don't."

"No, ma'am."

"That's all right," she said. "As long as you get the names and places right, I don't mind the color. You just keep on bringing me the news."

And I did that all the time I worked for Miz Mulrooney, telling her everything I heard. There was only once I held something back and that was mostly by accident.

I was upstairs sweeping up the mud and grit the miners tracked into the dormitory when I came across a magazine under one of the beds. It was filled with stories about adventures and danger. I hadn't had anything new to read for so long, there didn't seem no harm in sitting down to have a quick look. After all, I worked pretty steady most of the time. But just in case, I slouched down on the floor behind one of the curtains. I was in the middle of a ripping good story when there was the clump of boots on the stairs and voices. Some fellows seemed to be having an argument, which got fiercer as they came into the room, close to where I was. What struck me at first was the way one of them spoke. His accent was pretty heavy, and it took some listening before you was sure it was English.

"I tell you, yust look up at da hillside, da vay she slopes and her ridges go crosswise, like a terrace."

The other person just grunted and sat down on one of the beds.

"You know vat I tink?" said the first one. "I tink maybe liddle rivers run along dere in old days."

"That don't mean beans, Axel."

"Vat is harm digging dere? One shaft?"

"It's a blame fool idea, that's the harm," said the other one. "Nobody's digging on the hills. Tell you the truth, I'm ready to give up and find a job with somebody who knows what he's doing and can pay me wages."

"You do if you vant," said the first one, "but maybe you lose out and I get rich."

That made the second one laugh, although not very

hearty. There were sounds of other people on the stairs, and the two stopped talking. I peered around the curtain and saw them lying on their bunks with their feet hanging over the edge, which was Miz Mulrooney's rule—no boots on the beds. One of the men was wearing a peaked red cap that tied under his chin, like a nightcap. "Tink about it," he said to the other fellow, who had a black checked cap set over his face. Other men came in then and stomped around and complained in general about the life they was leading. I slipped the magazine back where I found it, crept out with my broom, and made like I was finishing up a corner, but it didn't matter, because nobody paid me any mind.

I had made a report to Miz Mulrooney earlier that day, so I didn't tell her about the two men. Probably I wouldn't have anyway. They was just two prospectors wore out from digging for gold and not finding any, like Pa and Jack and the rest of us. I might not've even remembered them at all, if a couple days later I hadn't seen the man with the red cap and his partner on one of the round hills above Skookum Gulch. Both of them were swinging their pickaxes, so I figured that Red Cap must've won the argument.

Two days after that he came down in the middle of the day and passed right by Grand Forks Hotel on the trail to Dawson. I noted him as a man who walked like he had a purpose in mind and somewhere to go. Miz Mulrooney was gone to Dawson herself right then, looking to build another hotel, so I didn't worry whether I should report to her what I saw.

That evening when I got back to the cabin, Pa was sitting with his feet in a basin of water. He looked so downhearted that I made a story out of what I'd heard from Red Cap and his friend. I tried to mimic the accent. "Says he vants to dig vere dere might be liddle rivers from old days."

"That so?" Pa said, not even lifting his head.

"But he must've changed his mind about the whole thing, because I saw him this morning going hell-for-leather toward Dawson."

"Now, Billy," Pa said, without much spirit, "your ma wouldn't like to hear you use such language."

"That's the only way to describe how he was tearing along, Pa."

Jack was stacking a load of stove wood. He put each log down careful-like, as if it had to be just so. "Hmm," he said. "Maybe Dawson wasn't his aim. Maybe he was headed to Forty Mile . . . to record a claim."

"Why, yes," I said. "That could be."

We stared at each other.

"What else did he say about the hillsides, Billy?"

"I don't recall exactly. He was trying to convince his partner that he knew something from the way the ridges run, like maybe they showed the paths of old creek beds."

Ed turned around from the kettle of beans she was boiling. "I've seen those fellows, too," she said, "one wearing a checked cap and the other one red. They came down to Grand Forks yesterday and begged enough lumber scraps to make a rocker and didn't have money to pay for it. They seemed real anxious. You remember I told you, Jack?"

He nodded. "There could be old stream beds up there, I suppose."

While we was cleaning up after supper, Jack said, "It wouldn't hurt us to look for the kind of ridges that watercourses leave behind, would it, Gip?"

"Sounds far-fetched," Pa said as he worked over his sore feet with a piece of rag. "But I wouldn't mind a spell of doing something other than digging in the dark, twelve feet down and nothing but plain dirt to show for it."

Ed wanted to know had I reported this information to Miz Mulrooney.

"I would've probably, but she's gone to Dawson to talk with folks about building another hotel."

"Good," she said. Her eyes had lit up, and she got that fierce look like she had when we was starting out, when she knew we was going to strike it rich. "Keep your ears open and your mouth shut, Billy."

Sure, I thought, *just like a no-vote member of this crew, even if I did bring them the information.*

Next day she and Pa and Jack went exploring, not where Red Cap and his partner had been working but on the opposite slope of Skookum Gulch. I should keep on working for Miz Mulrooney, they said, and not arouse curiosity about what we was doing.

I did hear more about the man in the red cap—his name, it turned out, was Axel Clausen. He and his partner had made a bench claim, which was what folks called claims that weren't in the creek bed. The old-timers sitting around Grand Forks Hotel laughed fit to bust over the idea of digging on the hills instead of down where the real streams run. I was half ashamed they'd see my folks up there doing the same, so I did keep my mouth shut and went on sweeping and chopping wood, while Jack and Ed and Pa poked around on the hillside and dug some test holes.

The first two shafts didn't produce anything. But Jack got it in his head that if there were old stream beds like Axel and his partner were supposed to have found on that side of Skookum Gulch, there must be some on the other side, too.

Pa had high hopes at the beginning of the bench digs, but those two shafts took the starch right out of him.

"I don't know but that we're acting the fools up there," he said, "just like folks think."

"Maybe," Jack said. "Still, I got a hunch, Gip, that we're on a good track this time."

"Me, too," my sister chimed in.

Well, I thought, *anytime you go counting on hunches from Edna Rose McGee, you're in trouble.* "What about that fraction claim you was so sure of?" I asked, and Ed gave me one of her glares.

"What's done is done," Pa said. "On this hunch I'll give you one more shaft. If that don't produce something, Jack and I should start looking for work on someone else's claim."

"All right, Pa," Ed said. "Give us one more, and if that don't show pay dirt, I'll get a job with the Mary Belle Laundry and you and Jack can hire out."

So they was all agreed and had long discussions about where to sink that last shaft. I don't know who won out because I was still working down at Grand Forks the day they started it.

It was maybe two, three days later that Jack came into the dining room where I was sweeping up. He sat down at the bar and said he'd have coffee if it was still on the stove. When the barkeep went to fetch it, Jack whispered I should come along to Skookum Hill just as soon as I could skedaddle.

"We've hit something," he said. "Keep it under your hat." The man came back with a mug of coffee that had been boiled all morning, but Jack drank it down and gabbed about one thing or another and then said he had to be off. I kept on sweeping.

It was staying light quite a bit longer by then, and I could see Jack and my sister up on the eastern bench of Skookum Hill almost as soon as I crossed over the Bonanza. They was working above a little stream that angled down and emptied into the gulch creek when it was running, which it soon would be. I hiked uphill toward them, hollering, "Any luck?" before I remembered.

Jack shouted over his shoulder, "Not much, Billy. Your pa has already called it a day. Me and Miz McGee are just cleaning up."

When I got close, Ed grabbed me in a hug and then shook me good. "We're trying to keep this quiet, Billy, so don't go shouting like that." Then she turned to Jack. "Show him," she said.

Jack gestured I should come close to where he was dumping dirt behind a clump of rabbit brush. "Look here," he said, pulling his hand out of his overalls pocket, and there was two nuggets, one of 'em as big as a hazelnut.

"Whoopee! Where'd that come from?"

"The last shaft, Billy, the one we had the hunch on, me and your sister. Two, three feet down we hit white gravel with little bits of gold you could see, and then these turned up. Your pa has gone back to the cabin with a couple buckets of dirt to pan out. We look to have made a strike, Billy, my friend."

"Whoopee!" I said again, fingering the nuggets, feeling how solid and heavy they was. "Ain't it lucky I heard that Axel fella talking?"

"Now, don't you go blabbing," Ed said. "We don't want other folks up here digging before we stake our claim."

The two of them was so excited they could hardly keep to the path on the way back. They kept jostling one another and guessing how much Pa would pan out and who should go to Forty Mile to register the claim.

"It'll have to be Jack," I said. "You can't make a claim, Ed, because you ain't eighteen, if they'd even let a girl do it anyway, which I doubt. And Pa already made his claim for that fraction you was so cocksure about."

Jack gave me one of his crooked smiles, but my sister didn't seem to care. After telling me not to go whooping and hollering, she was pretty close to that herself, even more so after we got to the cabin and Pa showed us what he got from panning the buckets—a little pile of gold flakes.

"Could be ten, maybe fifteen dollars," he said. "If they're all like that, we'll make our fortunes on Skookum Hill. Of course, this might be a fluke." But you could tell he didn't believe it was. He looked like about ten years had slid right off, and more like his old self that he'd been before Ma died.

Ed, she hurrahed and grabbed him by the hand and made him whirl around the cabin, knocking into tree stumps and hanging laundry. Jack did one of his jigs, feet going ever which way. Then he grabbed Ed's hand and they went spinning around together. It was something to see, how a little pile of gold flakes and a couple nuggets could change people.

"Might just be a fluke," I said, and stayed put.

Of course, I hoped it wasn't and that we was on our way to striking it rich. I had it in mind to buy the biggest, grandest stone available to mark Ma's grave.

But the way Ed and Jack and even Pa were all carrying on—like it was their hunch that led to the strike and my information had nothing to do with it—well, that just stuck in my craw. So I kept quiet, exactly like Ed wanted. Just like I'd been doing ever since they sold Persey.

Pa said I had to help at the claim while Jack was gone to record it, so I told Miz Mulrooney that I couldn't work for her for a few days. She had already heard about the claim somehow and wanted to know how it had come to us to sink a shaft on the hillside. I fudged a little, saying Pa's partner knew something about the way creeks likely changed course over the years, which was true. He just might not've recalled that without my telling what I had heard in Miz Mulrooney's second-floor dormitory.

"Hmm," she said, looking at me sharp through her spectacles. "A lucky guess, sounds like, and you folks deserve it more than most. I know your papa isn't going to gamble away his earnings or waste them on drink and the high life."

"No, ma'am, he won't do that."

"Good thing most prospectors don't feel that way, or some of us would have a harder time making a living," she said with a small smile. "Go along, Billy. Help your papa and come back when you can."

I did plan to go back. Chopping wood, sweeping floors, and listening to folks talk was a heck of a lot better than digging up froze dirt. But even after Jack got back, Pa said they needed me at the claim.

"What about my getting paid in grub, Pa? How are we gonna do without that?"

"We have enough now, Billy," Ed said, "and money to buy more if need be."

"But what if there ain't any to buy?"

"Seems like you're trying to get out of the hard work," Pa said.

"No, I'm not, but I'm doing good at that job, and Miz Mulrooney is counting on me."

"You tell Miz Mulrooney much obliged, only now you're going to work with your folks. Do you hear me, son?"

"Sure, Pa," I said.

Miz Mulrooney wasn't as broke up over my leaving as I had hoped, but she wasn't happy, neither. "Well, I'm sorry to lose you, Billy McGee, as you are my best reporter. Drop by when you can, and if you come across anything you think would interest me, bring it along."

"Yes, ma'am," I said.

I didn't hear much to report on, of course, since I spent most of my days in a hole, thawing and digging out buckets of dirt and hauling them up by the windlass—backbreaking work. It was eased now and then by the glint of gold flakes in the dump and looking forward to the time when the streams would run again. Then we, and everyone else up and down the valleys, could wash out the winter's haul. We dug until we got to bedrock and then drifted along to the side, following the old creek channel to the end of our claim and picking up nuggets as we went along. Not a nugget every day, but often enough to keep a person on the lookout and ready to crow. That first strike wasn't a fluke after all.

In fact, ours and Axel's and a couple other bench claims turned out to be about the last of the really good strikes made in the Bonanza Valley. Most of the old-timers thought all bench strikes were some sort of accident. They held firm to the idea that all the talk about old stream beds was just bunkum and figured Axel and us and a few others had just got lucky. But by and by, the bag of nuggets Pa had stashed on a little shelf on top of the door frame in our cabin got fuller and fuller, and we all knew how many was in there from day to day.

I felt like the two, three nuggets I'd found ought to be mine to keep, but Pa said we were a partnership, the four of us, and everything was going into a common pot to be settled later. I looked to my sister to raise a fuss and remind Pa that the McGees had a two-thirds share, so if there were fifteen nuggets, ten belonged to us. When I brought that up, she said, "Oh, never mind, Billy. Pa and Jack'll work it all out."

"They don't need to work it out. You people done all that when we first got to Dawson—two thirds for McGees, remember? Surely we got enough to put some aside for Ma's gravestone right now."

"You planning to buy a stone up here and haul it back to Skagway?"

"Um, no," I said, not having thought it through.

"So we'll figure that out later. Don't worry."

But I did worry. It seemed like somebody was going to be cheated, and maybe it was me and maybe it was Ma, and maybe my sister, Ed, didn't care. And once that idea got into my head, it seemed to take root and grow on its own.

15

ED'S BIRTHDAY

OUR MA HAD ALWAYS TREATED US special on our birthdays. We didn't have to do chores at all, not even washing dishes or carrying in stove wood, and could lie around all day unless school was on. So on the morning of Ed's birthday I got up a little early, boiled the coffee, stirred up some flapjacks, and brought out a little jug of syrup I had begged off the Grand Forks cook.

Then I climbed up to her loft and pummeled the bedroll.

"Get up, lazybones. It's your turn to make the breakfast, ain't it?"

She rolled over, rubbing her eyes, looking peeved at being waked out of a sound sleep. "It's early yet, Billy. Leave me alone."

"Come on." I punched her again. "What do you think this is, your birthday?"

It took her a second before she caught on and smelled breakfast already cooking.

"Well, now, it might just be," she said, and her mouth kind of turned up.

Getting Ed to smile before breakfast was a near miracle. That's what Pa said as he hauled her out and gave her a little swat. We all sat down to have a good feed, as befit folks who had struck it rich and was celebrating a birthday to boot. Pa ruffled Ed's hair a little, which I supposed was the end of the birthday greetings, but then Jack stood up and said, "Wait a minute, now."

He went off and rummaged among his belongings, then brought out a small wood box, which he laid down on the plank table in front of Ed. It looked to be made of alder wood and had some sort of posy carved on the lid.

"Many happy returns," he said.

I knew my sister would scorn it, since she scorned everything that wasn't useful. I waited for her to say "Much obliged" in that cool way she had. Instead, she brushed her fingers over the carved lid and her face went red, like she'd been the one standing over the stove instead of me.

"Thank you," she said. Then she left the table and carried the box up to her loft. I felt a little sorry for Jack to be treated that way, when he'd gone to so much trouble to give her a present. But it just showed, again, how little he knew about us, how we didn't give presents much and that Ed was likely embarrassed, maybe even peeved. It served him right, but I thought I'd be friendly and explain things anyhow.

"Never mind about Ed," I said later, while we was working the windlass. "Maybe you don't know, but she don't care much for things that ain't useful. Where'd the box come from, anyway?"

He gave me one of his slanty-eyed looks. "I made it," he said. "You want me to show you how?"

"No," I said. "I don't take to that kind of thing."

We didn't talk any more about it, but still, I got a feeling something was going on.

When everyone was out of the cabin, I sneaked up to Ed's loft and had a good look at the box. There was a rose carved in the lid, not a good one like I would have for Ma's gravestone, but still you knew it was a rose. Inside the box was some gewgaws—a necklace made of shells, old buttons, a little carved figure that looked like someone in a big hat, and Ma's locket. All of it, except the locket, was the sort of stuff Ed didn't give a hoot for. I fingered the carving, wondering where it came from, and thought about the tin box we buried behind the tent cabin with my tin soldiers and Ma's things that Ed said wasn't useful so we had to leave behind. How come now she had that very same kind of stuff in Jack Purdy's box?

I was still worrying over that a couple evenings later when Missus Mary Belle Gruber of the laundry place came to visit, bringing a pie made from dried apples.

"Seems like I heard there was a birthday around this time," she said, smiling at Pa as if he was the one with the birthday. "I had this extry and thought you might enjoy it, Mr. McGee."

"It ain't his birthday," I said. "It was my sister's, but that was a couple of days back, so you're too late."

Ed put a hand on my arm and squeezed hard. You could almost call it a pinch. "It don't matter about the day, Missus Gruber, and thank you. Won't you sit down with us and have a slice?"

"Don't mind if I do," Missus Gruber said. Next thing I knew there was coffee boiled up and people sitting around the plank table talking away like anything. Missus Gruber seemed to direct most of her remarks to Pa. It was embarrassing to see, though we was all polite, even Ed.

As soon as Missus G. was out the door, picking her way across the mess of lumber and flumes and sluice boxes that lay between our place and the Grand Forks trail, I said, "What makes her think she can come over here and take up our evening?"

They all looked at me as if I had cleared out my nose without a handkerchief.

"I swear I don't know what's gotten into you lately. Seems like you're turning mean," Ed said. "Missus Gruber was just being friendly."

"Huh," I said, thinking that Ed used to be the one to complain about nosy neighbors. *She* was the one who was changing her stripes.

A few days later I came across more proof of that. Jack and Pa had built a flume on the hill to divert a little stream so it would run through the sluice boxes, which Pa had commenced to make in a sort of work area he had set up in one corner of the cabin. Whenever he needed more supplies, I got sent down to Grand Forks to the lumber place. On that day Pa was short of nails, so I went on down, glad of being on my own, with the chance of seeing Miz Mulrooney, not that I had any news. She seemed pleased to see me, but was in the middle of some business talk with one of her partners, so I wandered off and stopped in at the shed where she let folks house their dogs.

It was late when I started back toward the cabin, but with days getting longer there was a nice long twilight. I decided to circle around to our claim even though Pa needed the nails back at the cabin. Ed or Jack might still be there, and I'd have somebody to walk home with. Sure enough, both of 'em was on the hill. But they weren't working. They was sitting together on the flume box with their backs toward me. When I got closer, I saw that Jack Purdy had his arm around my sister. I felt like I had been struck a blow right where I breathe or even that I had somehow passed out for a second and wasn't seeing right. When I looked again, they was still sitting there, staring out at where the sun was going down—my sister, Ed, and Jack Purdy. Then she turned toward him and laid her head right down against his shoulder.

I spun around and, without making any noise, went creeping off slantwise back to the trail that ran along the Eldorado. By and by I found a stump and sat a while trying to make sense of what I seen. Could it be they had been playing tricks all this time, acting like they hated each other? Or maybe they had stopped hating each other. . . . But when did that happen?

I went back over the time we had been together, from the very beginning on Chilkoot Pass to this very point, and I couldn't see any other answer except they were both liars. It seemed that just when you got used to a person being who that person let on to be, you found out that all the time the person was secretly being someone else. That was the worst kind of lying, in my book.

After a spell I got off the stump and went back to the cabin. Pa was pretty cross, as he'd been waiting for me all afternoon. Now, he said, it was near too late to work and he was riled. "Me, too," I wanted to say, but did not.

The next day I asked if I could stay at the cabin and help him with the sluice boxes. We worked together without saying much for half the morning, while I worried how to put what needed to be said. I figured Pa was bound to understand, but still, you had to say things careful, especially if you was telling on somebody.

"When do you reckon we can clear outta here and go back to Skagway, Pa?" I asked to begin with.

"Skagway?" he said, like he had forgotten that place.

"Where Ma is buried."

He hammered in a couple more nails before he answered. "Poor Rose Ellen. It was mostly her idea, you know, us coming north to hunt for gold, and she's the one didn't make it."

"I know that, Pa. Remember how she said when we struck it rich, we'd go back to Tacoma and buy ourselves a farm? She must be looking for us to do that pretty soon. Surely we got enough nuggets."

"Not yet, Billy, not nearly, and recollect we're sharing with Jack."

"Yes," I said, "that's part of the trouble."

"Trouble?" He looked up from his nailing. "Something wrong?"

I considered whether to tell how I seen Jack and my sister sitting on the flume box with their arms around each other. "Not exactly, Pa, but me and Ed promised as soon as we struck it rich, we'd go back to Skagway and get a gravestone put up for Ma, so's folks would know who's lying there."

"We know, son."

"No," I said, "you don't. You never even seen her grave."

He straightened up from his work, hammer still in his hand, and gave me such a look as made me drop my eyes. "You saying I don't mourn my wife, Billy McGee? Is that what you think?"

"No, no, Pa, I don't think that."

That's what I spoke, but I thought different. Seemed like I was the only one who really called her to mind and said her name out loud from time to time.

He went back to working on the sluice boxes and was quiet awhile.

"We will go, son," he said finally. "As soon as we play out this claim. But we can't leave before we run our dump through the sluices. Your ma wouldn't forgive me if I didn't get as much as I could from this trek, after all we've been through. I'm surprised you don't know that, without my saying."

"You aren't figuring on staying here all summer, are you, Pa?"

"We might. Jack says it's going to take some time to wash out what we got, and he thinks there's likely more pay dirt in the shaft."

"How come you take what Jack says for gospel truth, Pa?"

"What is eating you, Billy? Seems lately you got a lot of complaints about the family."

"Jack ain't family."

"Now, that's a turnabout. He looked to be your best friend when we left Lake Bennett."

"Yes," I said. "And my sister was dead set against him, but not anymore. Don't that make you wonder, Pa, what ails her, acting like she's getting sweet on a man we don't know nothing about?"

"I'll tell you what I wonder, and that's what's ailing

you, son. We have struck pay dirt, a miracle, but that's not enough for you. No, you got to make charges against your pa for not recalling his own dead wife, and your sister for breaking promises maybe she didn't even make. And Jack, who used to be was your friend and who we couldn't do without, him you charge with Lord knows what scoundrel intent. Ain't that so, Billy?"

It was so, but that didn't mean it wasn't true. Only I didn't know how to say that to Pa, so I just ducked my head and went back to working.

After a bit he sighed and said he hoped I would get over whatever was stuck in my craw.

"Don't worry about me, Pa," I said. "I'll be fine."

16

GARR AND THE TEAM

IT WAS GETTING TO BE SPRING, with longer days. Some willow branches had that gold-red look they get when they're about to push out their leaves, and you could hear the first trickle of melting snow running off hillsides—the thing everybody had been waiting for. People stomped around in gum boots with their coats and jackets hanging open and even gave out some cheerful hellos. Pa and Ed and Jack, they turned cheerful, too. All except me, and I didn't know exactly why.

It must've been then that I begun to think of going back to Skagway on my own, where I could be my own boss and choose my own job instead of having three people telling me what to do and how to feel. I took to looking for any excuse to leave Pa and them and go down to Grand Forks. Usually I went for supplies. Other times I said Miz Mulrooney was desperate for me to help out—and sometimes that was true, too. But she was more and more in Dawson planning her new hotel, so there was no one to bring news to. Still, I could always visit the dogs.

Miz Mulrooney thought a good deal of dogs and insisted on having a decent place for them when people came through with their teams. She had a big old dog called Nero, who could haul her in a sled back and forth to Dawson. She treated Nero like he was a human friend, but she was good to all the dogs and gave me leave to visit the kennels whenever I wanted. I would ask could I feed or water whichever dogs were there, and I'd try to make friends with 'em. That's not so easy with sled dogs, but some of 'em were never bred to be hauling goods and were in need of a little attention. I'd sit down with my arms around a poor old worn-out shepherd dog's neck and feel sorry for the both of us.

I was there one afternoon, sitting in the half dark, when the plank door was jerked open. A fellow stood against the light so all you could see was his big shape.

"Hey, kennel boy!" he yelled. "I got a bunch of hungry animals need grub right now."

I stood up, blinking, and came out into the hotel yard. The fellow was unharnessing a ragged-looking team from a sled, both dogs and gear clotted with muddy snow. The dogs circled around yapping, and the man laid the tail end of a harness into them, yelling they should shut up. One dog didn't yap or move, even when the harness was taken off, but stood alone, quiet except for snapping when one of the other dogs came too close. I would have known her anywhere, even as dirty and scrawny as she was.

"Hullo, Persey," I said, and I went right down on my knees in front of her with my hand out.

"Hey, kid, leave that dog alone. She'll take your throat out." The man grabbed her collar and tried to drag her off. "You don't want to be putting your hand out to a dog like that. She'll kill you."

"No, she won't, mister. She used to be my dog."

"I don't care if she was the Queen of England's dog. She's a mean animal." He whacked her a little with a harness end and she reared back, snarling. "See?"

He himself was mean looking, too—tall, with a black beard that started right below his eyes.

"You just come in, mister?" I asked, watching Persey, who had moved off a little ways.

"Come in from Skagway in two weeks and three days—beat my own record. Could you get a move on with the grub and water?"

His dogs crowded around for the scraps of meat, but just like always Persey took her share first. I waited until she was finished and then put my hand out so she could sniff it and remember who I was. She wouldn't wag her tail—she was too proud for that—but she looked up at me, and I knew she knew. So I put my arms around her and laid my face in her smelly fur.

"What'd you give her?" the man asked. "She won't let anyone hang on her neck like that."

"We was always friends, Persey and me," I said.

"Well, your view of her nature sure isn't the same as mine. She's a good lead dog, all right, but has to do everything her own way. Even if you beat her, it don't change her opinion. I've had a mind to dump her, but the others won't go without her, so I'm stuck with her, for this season, anyway."

"Where'd you get her, mister?"

"Bought her and the rest off some men in Skagway. But they're not for sale now, kiddo. I aim to beat my own time with 'em goin' south."

"Back to Skagway?"

"Gonna take the mail out one more time before breakup."

"Kinda late in the year for a sled, ain't it?"

"Ha," he said. "That's what the loafers sitting around Dawson think, but I know ice on the Yukon better'n any man alive."

That's when the thought popped into my mind, like it had been waiting all along.

"I'll bet you need someone to go along with you and look after the dogs." I thought he might laugh, and he did, while squinting at me.

"You have anybody in mind, kiddo?"

"Me," I said. "I'm real good with the dogs."

"I already have a partner," he said, "getting doctored over in Dawson right now. We don't need any extra baggage." But he kept on looking at me with his snow-burned eyes slitted up above the beard. "What's a young fella like you doing here on your own?"

I told him I was an orphan and was joined up with some prospectors further along the Eldorado. Both those things were part true, but the next part was pure malarkey. The way it came out so smooth surprised me. "We been looking for a way to get back to Skagway and get in touch with our business folks. This would be a good chance to do that," I said, holding tight to Persey. "Likely she won't give you no trouble if I'm along, mister."

"Well," he said after a long silence, "you might be worth taking as a passenger, but you'd have to pay for a share of the grub besides taking care of the dogs and keeping this one in line."

"I could take care of the dogs easy, mister. I don't know about paying."

He shrugged. "That would have to be the deal. How did your partners figure you were gonna get to Skagway, anyhow?"

I went on petting Persey. "They figured whoever went out would work his way."

"Well, you'd be doing that, too, but I'll need to have something toward your grub, you being an extra person."

I thought about the leather poke back at the cabin. Last count, there was near twenty nuggets. Some of them was surely my share.

"Well, I dunno," I said. "My partners might agree to that. How much would you want? I don't eat a lot."

"You will on this trip, kiddo. I aim to make a record

going south, beat my own time. You'll need to keep up, running alongside the team."

"A nugget would probably more than pay for my eats, mister," I said.

He looked at me close and grinned, his teeth showing bright in that black beard. "Sure, kid, a nugget might do it. I'd have to see the size, of course."

I was thinking as fast as I could while I petted Persey, and she stood there kind of patient, putting up with it. "I couldn't pay you until tomorrow."

"Well, that might be too late, kiddo. I'm leaving here first thing in the morning, headed for Dawson and then upriver."

Persey lifted her head and looked at me. I made up my mind right then. "All right, mister. I'll be here with a nugget."

The man said his name was Garr. He was planning to leave Grand Forks soon after sunrise, and I should be at the dog kennels then with my gear and pay for the trip. He wasn't going to wait on me, did I understand?

"Sure thing, Mr. Garr."

I was getting jittery, not only for what I was planning to do, but that Miz Mulrooney would come out back and ask after my folks and skew my story. We herded the dogs into the kennel and I hugged Persey, putting my mouth close to her ear. "You and me are going on a trip together." It seemed like she wagged her tail, but I couldn't tell for certain.

I walked back toward the cabin, working on my

reasons for skipping out. Ed had never stopped bossing me since we left Skagway—that was one thing. Then she stole Jack, who was my friend first and who she said she hated. And after that she and Pa and Jack, all three, sold my dog. And then they treated me as if I didn't have a say in anything, and Pa made me quit working for Miz Mulrooney. Well, Miz Mulrooney was mostly gone now, so that one didn't hold up as much. But the rest of my reasons did. It seemed like there was nothing purely mine, but if I took this chance to run off, there would be. I'd go back to Skagway and dig up the tin box me and Ed had left behind, and somehow I'd get a gravestone for Ma, like we promised. It was only fair for me to have some of the nuggets, too—my share, anyway, because I was the one who heard Axel talking about a bench claim and that was how we came to strike it rich. But did anyone ever say, "Billy, this was all your idea, wasn't it?" No, they just kept on telling me what to do.

I figured it this way—the agreement was that McGees got two thirds, so that would be twelve nuggets and one left over. Who could argue that I didn't deserve a third of the McGee share? Of course, I couldn't come right out and ask for it. But if I could get back to the cabin before anyone else, I might be able to put my hands on that leather poke.

In the midst of all my thinking and planning, I heard a shout, and tarnation, there was Jack Purdy yelling at me from our dig on Skookum Hill.

"Come on up here, Billy, and lend a hand!"

Nothing for it but I had to turn off the trail and scramble up the hillside.

"Where've you been?" Jack asked when I got closer. "Seems like you're always missing just when we need help."

I muttered something about Miz Mulrooney, but he was too excited to listen. They had come to what seemed like a fork in the old streambed, where it went off in a different direction, and in the first bucketful along that route Pa had found three hunks of gold. "Like picking it off the street," Jack said. "I never thought I'd see one of those stories come to be true."

He hustled me along, not giving Ed time to complain about my being gone, and said I was to help Pa at the bottom of the shaft, where he had found yet another nugget, not as big as the first three but, as he called it, "respectable."

We worked until the light faded, and I figured my chance of running away was going down with the sun. I drug along behind the rest of them on the way back to the cabin, thinking about Persey and wondering if I could somehow take her back.

It was Jack's turn to do supper and he started right in, with Ed's help. We all took turns cooking, true to that agreement at Lake Bennett, which seemed so long ago and so wrong-headed to me now.

Pa cleaned off the new chunks of gold and laid them on the table. "Look at that. And considerable more to come when we wash out the dump, I'll wager. Billy, bring my notebook so's I can make a record. We had nineteen," he said after he opened the book, "and these four makes twenty-three. We'll probably quit counting pretty soon and just drop 'em in a bucket, like they do up at the Berry mine. I hear that whenever Missus Berry needs to buy something, she just sallies out to the dig and grabs herself a couple of nuggets. Billy, you can put these in the poke with the rest."

"You want me to bring the poke down, Pa?" I was in a kind of sweat and had to rub my hands against my pant legs.

"No, just drop 'em in, and I'll get our log written up. Then I aim to have a foot soak. Don't know what ails my feet, now that things are going good. Maybe it's the weather and they've swelled up like the buds on the trees, eh?" He gave me a quirky smile as he handed me the four new nuggets.

I was thinking, *Why don't you mention Ma and Skagway and buying back my dog like you promised?* but I didn't peep a word. I just took the nuggets and hauled a stump over to the doorway, stood on it, and reached for Pa's old leather purse that we called a poke now and was where we kept our hoard. Nineteen and four made twenty-three, and two thirds of that is just about fifteen. Five should be my share, but I thought I'd make it four, to be really fair. Then, on second thought, I made it five, as I didn't know what a gravestone would cost. I fingered five nuggets out of the poke, put 'em in my pocket, and dropped the clean new ones inside. Then it seemed like everything stopped for a second while I stood there with my knees quivering, waiting for someone to grab me or say, "Billy, what are you doing with those nuggets in your pocket?"

The murmurs of Ed and Jack went on, along with the sounds of beans boiling and wood snapping in the stove. I turned around real slow and stood there looking down—it seemed like from a great ways off—at my pa and sister and Jack Purdy. Ed and Jack was arguing about how much salt pork to put in the beans, and Pa was working on his notebook. No one looked up at me. I felt invisible, like I could've thumbed my nose or stuck out my tongue or danced a jig on the stool with the nuggets rattling in my pocket and nobody would notice.

I didn't do any of that, of course, only stood there rocking a little and looking down at them. When Pa moved the lantern closer to his writing, he glanced up at me with a little smile and went back to scribbling. I cinched up the drawstring on the poke, put it back where I'd found it, and jumped down.

After supper I said I had promised Miz Mulrooney to help with a dog team early in the morning, although it shouldn't take long.

"Whoa," Ed said. "You can't just be taking off all the time this way, Billy. We need you at the claim."

"But I promised," I said, "and I can't let her down after she's done us favors with grub and all."

"It does seem you've been slacking off lately," Pa said.

"I got to keep my word, don't I?"

Pa was a great one for standing by your word, so he said, "Well, maybe this once, but don't promise again. You owe time to your family, you know."

"Sure, Pa."

I climbed up to my loft early, rolled some clothes into an extra blanket, and sewed the nuggets into a pocket in my shirt. Then I lay down and tried not to think about what I had done and what I seemed bound to do the next day—run off from my folks and be my own boss after taking gold that maybe didn't really belong to me. But if I hadn't been meant to do it, it wouldn't have come so easy, I told myself. Besides, they didn't really need me. And on top of that, I had a chance to be with my dog that they had sold away.

When the first gray light came through our canvas windows, I was up and creeping out with my bedroll. The door creaked when I opened it, and Pa raised up.

"You're off mighty early, son."

"See you later, Pa," I said, and ducked out, my heart pounding. I sat for a moment on our front step to get my boots laced up and my bundle tight. Then I was off, half running over the frosty ground, the sky lighting behind me. The sun was still only making a glow on the hills when I came into the hotel yard. Mr. Garr was already there, packing his sled with provisions.

He gave me a look like he was surprised I had showed up. "Well," he said, "appears I got company mushing down to Skagway, after all. What's your name, kiddo, and where's your grub money?"

"Um," I said, trying to figure out how to get at my store of nuggets without him seeing where I kept 'em. "You can call me Tacoma Kid."

If you was to ask me where I got that name right then while I was hunched over, pretending to be digging into my boots instead of fiddling around in my inside pocket, I wouldn't be able to tell you. I couldn't even look around until finally I had a nugget in my hand.

He took the nugget and squinted at it. "All right," he said, "I guess this'll cover most of your grub. But you'll have to work for the rest of it by looking after the dogs."

"Yes, sir, Mr. Garr."

"Now, make yourself useful and get the team harnessed up."

Persey knew exactly what she was supposed to do as soon as she saw the harness, but maybe it looked like I was giving her orders, because she stood meekly while I buckled her in and hooked her to the gang line. Now that I was closer to the rest of the team, it seemed like some were familiar and others not. But they all was willing to follow Persey.

We was ready to go before Mr. Garr had drunk his mug of coffee in the hotel kitchen. When he came out with his last load of stuff, Miz Mulrooney came along behind him and stood looking out over the Eldorado Valley in the dawn light.

I ducked down behind the sled, pretending to be checking the ropes.

"Seems foolish to set out for Skagway by sled this time of year, Mr. Garr," she said, "but if you're determined to do so, I'll trust you with those orders for goods for my new hotel in Dawson."

"You can count on me, ma'am," he said. "I'll be in Skagway two weeks from today or know the reason why." He took up his long-handled whip. "Here we go."

"Mush on, Persey," I said into her ear, keeping myself half crouched as I jogged alongside the dogs. Persey took off with a burst of speed, so we was clean out of the hotel yard when Miz Mulrooney called, "Who's that with you? Not one of my boys, I hope."

"The Tacoma Kid," Garr yelled as he snaked the whip over the backs of the team, only to show off, I reckoned, since Persey was running hell-bent, and the rest of the dogs with her.

17

MUSHING UPRIVER

WE HAD TO STOP in Dawson to pick up mail packets and to see about Mr. Garr's partner, who was ailing with scurvy. First, though, Mr. Garr stopped outside the Pioneer Saloon and told me to wait a minute with the dogs while he took care of some business. That minute turned into what seemed like an hour, and I worried that Pa and them would figure out what I'd done and come after me and I'd be hauled back to Grand Forks without ever getting farther than Dawson. I began to suspect that Mr. Garr was inside having a second breakfast. Since I hadn't had any breakfast at all, I figured I could join him.

I tied the dogs to a rail, except for Persey, and went and stood by the door, peering into the darkness until I could make out Mr. Garr. He was leaning against the bar, not eating, but jawing away to beat the band with a clutch of men. It seemed like he was the center of attention.

"Here's the odds, Garr," the barkeep said, pouring beer into a mug and handing it to him. "Ten-to-one you won't make Skagway before breakup."

"That's a sure-thing bet," said one old-timer. "With Sam laid up, it's for certain gonna take you longer, having to do everything yourself."

"I got Sam replaced," Mr. Garr said.

"With that kid?" someone hooted, and everyone laughed.

"Well, I suppose he won't eat much," said another.

"He knows how to handle the dogs, better than Sam or anyone else within spitting distance," Mr. Garr said, taking a swallow of the beer. "And nobody knows Yukon ice better 'n me. It's solid now and will stay like that all the way to Lake Bennett—you can put your money on it."

People began calling out dates in May and elbowing in to lay money on the bar, betting that Mr. Garr couldn't reach Skagway before breakup and guessing which day that was going to happen.

"Too chicken to put your own money on a date, Garr?" someone asked.

"So long as I'm in Skagway collecting my bonus, I don't give a hoot what day the river breaks up. I'm putting my stake on beating my own record, and I aim to win. Then I'll come back and get what you slackers owe me."

There was more joshing and shouting, and finally Mr. Garr turned around. Someone must have pointed me out. When he came toward me, glowering, I stepped back with my hand on Persey's collar. She growled and Mr. Garr brushed right on by.

"Didn't I tell you to wait with the team, Kid?"

"Yes, sir, but that was a while back and I ain't had breakfast yet." I was thinking about the nugget I'd paid for my grub and how many pancakes it would buy. I probably should've been thinking about other things, like how it seemed Mr. Garr knew all along that his partner was too sick for another trip and that's how come I got to take his place and pay for it besides. But by the time I figured all that out, my stomach was full of flapjacks and we was on the trail south and it seemed too late to complain.

After the Pioneer we picked up mailbags and packets and were on our way, mushing along the frozen river, in and out of the great ice heaves that Mr. Garr said he knew like the back of his hand. Sometimes I ran alongside with the dogs, and sometimes he let me ride while he handled the gee pole. It was hard work, but nothing compared to the misery of digging and hauling froze dirt all day on the claim. The idea that I was finally free of all that and on the way to being boss of my own life—well, it gave me a thrill, to be sure, and helped me to ignore the exhaustion that comes with running for hours on end.

At first we set up a little tent at night, but the further south we traveled, the milder the weather grew. Then we laid our blanket rolls on fresh-cut pine boughs and went to sleep looking up at the stars. In the mornings we was off as soon as the sky lightened enough to see to harness up the team. Being set as he was on beating his own record for going upriver, Mr. Garr kept us moving as fast as we could travel. He didn't waste much time in small talk, although he did ask once exactly why I was set on going to Skagway.

"Business," I said.

His eyes kind of lighted. "What kind of business, Kid?"

"Family business," I said, thinking the purchase of a gravestone was not likely to impress him.

"Well," he said, pulling out his pipe for a smoke before turning in, "whatever the business is, I guarantee to get you there in record time."

My job was to feed the dogs and look to their feet lest they get torn from running on ice. If they did, we had to stop and wrap the paws of whatever dog was leaving bloody prints. Mr. Garr grumbled at having to do that, but he knew we couldn't afford to lose even one of them.

At first we made good time, nearly flying, it seemed, down past Stewart River and the old man's cabin that was still there, dark and quiet in its grove of trees and no smoke coming from the chimney. It was midday, so there was no question of our stopping overnight. I was glad of that, afraid that Persey might somehow remember her old master and want to stick around. She kept her nose to the trail, though, and went right on.

As we sped over the snow, my mind kept coming back to thoughts of Pa and Jack and my sister, Ed—what they might be doing back at the cabin or if they was sorry I was gone. I sure didn't miss Ed's bossing or the way they all counted me as a no-vote one bit. But some nights, as me and Mr. Garr sat chewing on cold biscuits, I imagined them gathered round the plank table with a delicious hot meal and Jack telling one of his troll stories, and I almost felt regretful for what I done.

Spring seemed to be coming up to meet us. As we went along, more signs popped out—leaf buds swelling on the river willows and the alders, patches of new green where the snow had melted, and snowdrops and bluebells coming out in the sun. When it was real sunny, I took off my parka and ran along in the flannel shirt with the pocket where I'd sewed my nuggets. Sometimes I pretended to be scratching myself, just so I could feel them four nuggets safe and sound.

In spite of the warming days, ice on the river held pretty solid, even with the layer of slush on top that Mr. Garr probed carefully with his pole. He began to haul me out of my blanket roll even earlier then, so we could travel while it was still cold. By afternoon the slush was so thick, we usually had to leave the river and make our way along the bank. The going was terrible rough and slow there, which put him in a temper.

He cursed under his breath and laid his whip among the dogs. "Keep a move on, you mangy beasts," he'd growl. "You make me lose time and I'll see each one of you turned into dog meat." He railed worse even than Ed when she was in her prime. Of course I didn't make any remark, even with worrying about the dogs getting whipped. I figured I'd only make things worse, and best to keep moving as fast as I could and see that Persey did the same.

I was surprised at how well I could keep up, a lot better than when we had come along the same trail in the fall. Maybe winter at Grand Forks had hardened me—it must've been that, and being with Persey again. She wouldn't hardly glance my way when she was at work leading the team, but when the day was over and she'd had her feed, she let me pet her and would sit with me by the fire for a while.

Along about Hootalinqua, where the Teslin River comes in, Persey began to get skittish. Sometimes Mr. Garr had to use the whip pretty fierce to get her to lead the others out on the ice. He kept looking back, like someone was on our trail, but there never was anyone coming our way, nor going back the other way, neither. I reckoned they was all waiting for breakup to ride to Dawson on the river, those folks in the cabins and trading posts. Still, Mr. Garr would spin around from time to time and stare backward, muttering under his breath. He kept count of the days, and each one passing made him fiercer. Bad ice was slowing us down for sure, and finally, at Lake LaBarge, it seemed like we had come to the end of traveling on frozen water.

There was hardly any living with Mr. Garr then. He never did hit me, but he looked like he wanted to, and he laid his whip among the dogs more and more as they struggled over rough ground dragging that sled. When we was about halfway down the lake, there came a cold snap, and back we went on the ice. Although it was slushy by midday, it seemed firm underneath and we moved along pretty fast.

The next morning I rolled out as soon as Mr. Garr yelled and went down to the lakeshore to check the ice, the same as we did every day. He had a long pole he used to poke the ice all around. I didn't have a pole, so he'd told me to get myself one from a fallen tree, the longest I could manage to carry. If I ever hit an open spot and fell in, I should quick-like hold the branch horizontal, so its ends would rest on either side of the hole. That morning I grabbed the pole, looked out over the lake, and rubbed my eyes, trying to figure out if I was seeing things or if the ice was actually moving.

Mr. Garr said no. He had run this trail too many times to count and knew exactly what state the ice was in, but we had to move fast. Instead of breakfast, we chewed on some old corn cakes as we traveled.

At first it seemed that Mr. Garr was right and the ice was going to hold to the end of Lake LaBarge. But that didn't last. As the sun rose higher, the layer of water on top of the ice got deeper and what was underneath went soft. Shortly after noon Mr. Garr cursed up a storm and said we had to go back to the shore. Half the time we was stopped, trying to make our way around fallen trees and tangled roots. Mr. Garr jerked on the sled and roared at me and the dogs until he wore out his voice. Toward evening, as colder air came down on us, he called a halt and went down to the shore with his testing pole.

"We're going back on the lake," he shouted. "This ice'll hold us. Hurry up, we ain't got much daylight left."

When I tried to follow, Persey balked and dug her feet into the bank. Mr. Garr came back up with his whip in one hand and the pole in the other. "You make that damn dog do what I say or I'll lay into both of you." He whirled the whip around and made it crack above our heads. I dodged away, grabbed Persey's harness, and dragged her down the bank, staying with her at the head of the team. Mr. Garr ordered us to keep moving southward but to keep fairly close to shore. I thought maybe he was right and knew the ice better than anyone. As bad as it looked in the twilight, it felt pretty solid under my feet—that is, until the moment it began to shift.

At first the sway was so light, I thought I must've imagined it. Then I knew I hadn't. It was like stepping on a log you think is moored solid but begins to roll. I heard myself screaming, "Mr. Garr, the ice!"

He must've felt it, too. "Keep moving, for God's sake, boy! Head for shore."

Right then the ice ripped away, and a black hole opened in front of me and Persey. I dropped the pole and grabbed for my hunting knife even before I knew what it was I aimed to do. The ice was slipping away under our feet and the dark hole grew larger. It seemed to be going ahead of us, leaving no way to escape. As we came to the edge, I jerked on Persey's harness and stroked through the leather with my knife. Then her and me went tumbling down together into freezing black water, and after us the sled and the other dogs still harnessed to it.

I never saw nor touched the sled and other dogs again. I was turning over and over, and I didn't know which way was up until I saw the thick white ceiling above me. We seemed to be alone under the ice, Persey and me. *Hopeless,* I thought. *Can't get out of this one.* Persey was whipping around, her legs pumping furiously. I grabbed her collar as she twisted away, and suddenly we both came into the air. I took a big breath, and we went down and then came up again. This time I saw the shore and Mr. Garr waving wildly, his mouth open—yelling what, I couldn't hear. There was a shelf of ice between us and him that had a bright and jagged edge. I let go of Persey and paddled until I came up against it. She was beside me for a moment, then she was up above, scrambling away across the ice shelf.

Mr. Garr cupped his hands around his mouth and yelled, "Hitch yourself onto the ice, kiddo, real slow. That's right. Now spread out your arms."

I must've done that, somehow. I only remember the sharp edge of the ice cutting into me and taking my breath as I hung there, my legs dangling in the black water. Then suddenly there came the gee pole, quivering as it scooted across the ice. For a horrible second I thought Mr. Garr was going to stab me and send me back down to die.

"See the line on the end of the pole? Grab it quick."

I saw my hands swinging over the ice in a kind of half circle, like they didn't know where the gee pole was exactly or the rope fastened to it. I watched the hands come together and lay on top of the pole and then slip off.

"Try again," Mr. Garr yelled. "You can do it! Grab the line and come up out of the water, slow. Lie flat now, like I told you—easy, easy!"

I don't know how he talked me out of that hole in the ice, but seems like he did. I felt the sharp, jagged edge digging into me again, and then I was lying flat out.

"Put your arms through the loop in the rope and hang on. I'm gonna bring you in real slow." He hauled me across the rough ice, crouching and backing up as he pulled and talking the whole time. "That's it, you're doing fine. Slow and easy, kiddo."

Persey was already on shore, racing back and forth in a kind of frenzy. When I came close enough, she slithered down the bank and grabbed my parka in her teeth.

I don't remember anything more until I found myself wrapped in Mr. Garr's greatcoat, shaking hard, sitting by a fire that spit and sparked in the evening light. My clothes and boots was propped on sticks close by, and Persey was leaning up against me.

My gold nuggets! I had a sudden panic that they'd come loose while I was under water or, worse, that Garr had gotten hold of 'em. But then another bout of shivers hit me, and I had to put my arms round Persey for warmth.

It was a funny thing about Mr. Garr that I have puzzled over ever since. He had saved my life for sure, but instead of sitting back and being proud of that, he kept prowling around, shaking his head and muttering about the ice and how it had gone to pieces too soon. "Ten years on this river and I never seen it go like that. We must've had a late Chinook wind," he said one time. "You'd ought to thank your lucky stars I was watching close and saw the ice give way."

I stared at him. I thought I was the one that had felt the ice shifting under my feet. And hadn't it been *his* idea to go back on the lake that evening? It sure wasn't mine. But Mr. Garr acted like it was, or maybe somebody else's idea, we didn't know who.

While he was looking for a good stick to make a fishing pole, I reached over and felt my shirt. The weight of the nuggets was still there, and I relaxed some.

Mr. Garr hooked us some fish through the broken

ice and then fixed up our beds, and all that time he kept muttering and worrying about what had happened. By morning it seemed he had turned it all around to where it might even be my fault for running ahead with the team.

"I saved Persey," I said.

"Yeah, and almost drowned yourself for your trouble. You should never have been at the head of the team that way. And if you expect that mutt to thank you, you'll have a long wait, kiddo."

"I thank *you*, Mr. Garr," I said, "for hauling me out."

He looked kind of stunned for a moment, then he went back to grousing. "Yeah, and what about my dog team? And the mailbags that was gonna pay off a big bonus, and all that money laid on this trip? What about them?"

The more he thought about the fix he was in, and maybe even knowing it was his own fault, the more boiled up he got, trying to see a way to come out on top again. He was working it over in his mind, and by the time we got to the trading post at White Horse, he had made such a hard-luck story about our near drowning that the trader gave us food and gear on credit.

We went on by foot then, working our way toward Lake Bennett. A couple days later, when we came out on one of the bluffs and looked down on the lake, we saw a wondrous sight. There was such a parade of boats as you couldn't hardly dream of. Hundreds maybe, or thousands, waiting for breakup, which was likely to happen any day, as Mr. Garr and I had reason to know. We stood for a time, silent, and stared at all those boats—jammed along the shore or already out in the lake, scows and rafts, rowboats and barges, swirling about, sails ready to unfurl for the race downriver. The longer Mr. Garr stood there watching, the more cheerful he got.

"All those greenhorns and landlubbers heading for Miles Canyon and White Horse Rapids. What do you think they're gonna need, kiddo?"

"I don't know, Mr. Garr. Luck, I guess."

"More than that, Kid. They're gonna need a smart river pilot to get them through alive."

He swung what was left of his gear onto one shoulder and took off whistling.

I had to run a little to catch up. "You mean you aim to stay here, Mr. Garr?"

"So long as I can make money. And I will do just that, you can bet your boots."

"But aren't you going to go on to Skagway like we planned?"

"Skagway? What would I want to go to Skagway for without the mail packets? You want to go there, that's your lookout. Not me. I'll stay here, make my stake, then go back to Dawson. I advise you to do the same. Hitch a ride on a boat and work for your keep."

"I don't aim to go back to Dawson," I said. "I'm

going on to Skagway. I told you, I got business there."

He shrugged. "Suit yourself."

I swallowed and went on. "And I aim to take Persey with me."

"Oh, no you don't. That dog's my property."

"She don't like you, and she does like me, Mr. Garr. I need her."

"She's my property," he said again, looking at me with his eyes squinched narrow. "I paid for her."

"If I was to buy her off you, how would that be?"

"How you gonna do that, Kid?"

"Um," I said, fingering the four nuggets I had kept safe the whole time, nuggets to buy Ma's gravestone. Seemed like Garr hadn't noticed 'em when he pulled me out of the lake. Maybe two would be enough. I turned my back and fumbled around to get the nuggets free. "Here," I says, turning with two in my hand. "This should be fair."

His eyes narrowed even more. "You been holding out on me, kiddo. Never said a word about nuggets when I was begging credit at the trading post, no sir. Now you show up with two measly nuggets that ain't near enough for a lead sled dog."

"There's no snow," I said, "and no sled and no team, Mr. Garr. You going to take her on boats with you?"

"Don't get smart with me. I'll get paid fair and square or take her wherever I damn please."

I did my best arguing with him, pointing out that I'd paid for my share of the grub all the way to Skagway, but it wasn't no use. Somehow, he must've guessed how many nuggets there was. In the end I gave him everything I had and we parted company, him going down among the boats to rent himself out as a pilot and me and Persey headed south.

"Well," I said to Persey, "there's a man would make a good story. Started out mean, saved my life, and went back to being mean again. People surely can change, without giving notice." That brought to mind my sister, Ed, changing herself, and made me think of all them back at Grand Forks, maybe wondering where I was right at that moment.

"Come on, Persey," I said. "We'll make it on our own. I'll get a job. You know I got experience working for Miz Mulrooney. There'll be something like that—there has to be—and then we'll figure out a way to get Ma's gravestone."

Persey just kept trotting along, like she was still in harness, and I had to hustle to keep up with her.

18

A NEW JOB

FOR THE NEXT FEW DAYS I wandered around the south end of the lake, hiring myself out to chop wood for my eats and scraps for Persey. By then it seemed like there was an endless procession of gold hunters coming over White Pass and Chilkoot, and the hillsides clanged with the sounds of folks chopping down what trees was left to make more boats. The tent city was much bigger than the one I remembered. More frame buildings had sprung up, even a church on a bluff above the south shore. So many boats were moored on the lake, it looked like you could go halfway around just jumping from boat to boat and never touch ground nor water.

All those people were heading for Dawson, where all the good claims had been taken up long before. Of course, they didn't know that, and I sure wasn't going to cup my hands around my mouth and holler they might as well go on home. Let 'em discover that for themselves, I thought.

I was feeling a little grim. Except for Persey, I didn't have nothing to show for having run off with a share of my folks' nuggets. I had only the clothes on my back, and was having to ask for handouts to boot. I had to remind myself that I wasn't drowned dead in Lake LaBarge and ought to be thankful.

Finally, I got a job with a packer and his mule team going back down White Pass. Mr. Barker wanted someone to keep the animals from stumbling into the rotting carcasses of all the horses and mules that hadn't made it to the top—which was most of 'em, he said. In fact, folks were calling White Pass the "Dead Horse Trail."

It was a sorry sight, for sure. Sometimes me and Persey, coming along at the head of the mule train, had to turn away and think about something else instead of the bodies and bones of animals that had stumbled over boulders and broke their legs, or had fallen off cliffs and crashed to the bottom of ravines, or was so abused they just gave up and lay down to die.

In the evening as we sat around, Mr. Barker, who was much more sociable than Mr. Garr, told me what was going on in Skagway and how it was being ruled by a fellow named Smith.

"He's cock o' the walk down there," Mr. Barker said. "Him and his gang run everything: saloons, outfitters, hotels, and gambling halls. If you have any money, they smell it and get it off you before you're halfway up Broadway."

"There wasn't no cock o' the walk last summer."

"Well, there is now. Jefferson Smith is his name, but most folks call him Soapy, on account of a skin game he ran down in Colorado, where he took a five-dollar bill, wrapped it around a cake of soap, put another wrapper on that, then shuffled a half a dozen of those soap cakes on a little table. You had to pay a dollar to guess which one had the five. Course, no one ever did, unless it was the shill."

"I seen the same thing, only with walnuts, on the Chilkoot Trail," I said. "But those fellows wasn't running anything except their own game for people fool enough to fall for it."

"It's more than that in Skagway now. The businessmen and the town officers, nearly everybody, does what Soapy says. It's no skin off their noses, because the way he runs his gaming halls, it's mostly strangers that get cleaned out. In truth he isn't all bad. Had a benefit for the widows and orphans recently and was calling for a company of volunteers to go fight in Cuba. He gave money to build a school, too. Course, if you wondered where that money came from, that might keep you awake nights."

"Huh," I said. "I've met people who could relieve you of your money pretty quick." Then I felt a cold stab in my chest, thinking how I had relieved my very own family of some nuggets without a by-your-leave.

After we reached Skagway, Mr. Barker offered me supper and a bed in the hay for the night. "You can come on back and sleep in the barn anytime," he said, and I thanked him kindly.

The first thing I did the next morning was to go up to the cemetery. Ma's grave was just like it had been last time me and Ed stood looking down on it in the moonlight near a year before, a gravel mound without a marker. I stayed for a while, wondering if Ma had anything to say to me and if I did the right thing, coming back here on my own. But there was only the wind blowing through the trees, and after a while I whistled for Persey, and we went toward town.

I planned to sneak back around our old tent cabin to where we had buried the tin box. Someone was living in the cabin, of course, but worse, Missus Kettleson's place was still across the way with her old dog, Rusty, in the yard. I saw him coming, whapping his tail and getting ready to bark at Persey, so I scooted off. "Have to come back later," I said to Persey, "when Rusty ain't out."

We circled around and came into the main road, which they called Broadway now. It had been hardly more than muddy tracks the year before. Now it was lined on each side with wood buildings, and there was a boardwalk partway covering the street to keep you up off the mud. Nearly the whole of the valley was swept clean of trees. For green you had to look to the benches—long wooded ridges, like where we struck pay dirt up in Grand Forks—on either side of town.

I walked the full length of Skagway, just like Pa and me done in Dawson, and compared the two. You could match 'em one for one with saloons, it looked like, but Skagway had more shops selling stuff, and not just outfits. There was two cigar and tobacco shops, an assay office, some hotels, a gents' furnishing place, more eating houses, and gambling halls, too, of course. I didn't see a tombstone maker, but there had to be one somewhere.

"First thing is a job," I said to Persey after we got the lay of the land, "and some way to get grub." I figured I might find work at one of the eating houses, sweeping floors if nothing else, and was walking along trying to figure which one was the likeliest when I saw a man carrying a stack of newspapers. He went into Clancy's Saloon and then the Feed and Grain, and I could hear him calling, "Get your Skagway *Alaskan!*" He looked to have one leg shorter than the other and for that reason had a great deal of trouble hauling himself down off the boardwalk on one side and up on the other.

I tailed him awhile, and when he sat down on a log to rest, I came right out with what I had in mind, skipping over the restaurant business to newspaper work. Hadn't Miz Mulrooney said I was the best reporter she'd ever had?

"Hullo," I said, squatting beside him while he caught his breath. "Any jobs open in the news business?"

He gave me a long look. “This one,” he said, handing me the stack of papers. “You can hawk these up and down the street, if you’ve a mind.”

“How much does it pay?” I asked, thinking that newspaper offices probably didn’t have a lot of grub lying around.

“A percent of what you sell. Get rid of all these and you’ll have a couple of dollars, probably.”

That would do dinner for both me and Persey and then we could think further, so I said, “Okay, mister.”

“They call me Short Stack.” When he stood up right next to me, I saw why. “After you sell as many papers as you can, bring the proceeds to me at the *Alaskan*. It’s around the corner from the Golden North Hotel and right across from Jeff Smith’s Oyster Parlor.”

“Is he the one they call the Boss of Skagway?”

Short Stack had a round face with cheeks that looked like he’d stowed walnuts in ’em, and they bobbled when he spoke. “Some do, but don’t say I said so, and I wouldn’t advise you to go around mouthing it, neither. You’d better get moving if you want to get rid of these papers before midnight. Come around to the back of the office. I’ll be there in the pressroom setting up tomorrow’s edition.”

“Yes, sir, Mr. Short Stack,” I said, and me and Persey went off. The saloons and restaurants were pretty much like those in Dawson, maybe a little better built and some of the folks not quite as grubby looking. First I just scooted in and held out a paper to anyone who turned my way. Folks pushed me aside as they was getting to the gaming tables or elbowing in at the bar, and things went pretty slow. So I sat down on the boardwalk outside Harry's Pancake Palace and read through the paper, looking for something interesting.

In the next place I began to holler a little. "White Pass Railway moving along. Dead Horse Trail about to get a new name."

"That's old news, kid," some men said, but they laughed and bought a paper anyway. After I warmed up to it, I could tell when hollering would help business and when it wasn't so smart to interrupt a game of chance.

Short Stack seemed surprised when Persey and I showed up while it was still daylight.

"You're not finished this early, are you? Maybe dumped some papers off the wharf?"

"No, sir, Mr. Short Stack. I sold 'em all fair and square." I handed him the money I'd collected, and he counted it and gave me two bucks.

"Good work," he said. "If you're interested, come back tomorrow around noon and I'll have another stack for you." He turned back to a machine that made little clunking noises.

"What I'm interested in mostly is getting a reporting job," I said.

"How's that?"

"I have experience listening to what people say and then making it kind of lively. Might be good for your paper."

He swung around on the little stool he was using and fixed me with a hard stare.

"First place, it's not my paper. Second place, you're a mite big for your britches looking for reporting work. How old are you, anyhow?"

"Fifteen," I said, crossing my fingers. It was only a little stretch and not as old as me and Ed had got away with on Chilkoot Pass.

"Ha," he said. "Tell me another. What's your name?"

"Tacoma Kid."

"Your folks back in Tacoma?"

"No, sir." I paused, then said, "I'm an orphan," without even crossing my fingers, because my ma was dead and I had run away from what was left.

"Okay," he said. "Now we got more of the picture. You're looking for work, right?"

"Yes, sir, Mr. Short Stack."

"Aw, call me Shorty or don't call me nothing, Kid. The *Alaskan* has a reporter and probably don't need a boy standing around waiting for him to retire. You can go on hawking papers, though. It won't fetch you much, but'll keep you in eats. What else can you do?"

"Sweep floors and chop wood," I said.

"Hmm." He scratched his head so his bristly gray hair hopped around. "Maybe Mr. Bigelow would see his way clear to have you help out around the office—besides hawking papers, of course."

"Mr. Bigelow?"

"Owner and publisher of this fine example of journalism that you've been selling all afternoon. Let's go ask him. Better leave the dog behind."

He got up from his stool and motioned me to follow him through a door into what looked like the front office, with windows on the street where you could see Jeff Smith's parlor right across the way. In the office were two big roll-top desks, both open and showing all their little bins stuffed with papers, and some drawers that was overflowing with papers, too. A stout man in shirtsleeves with a vest that barely covered his front was hunched over one of the desks.

"I found us a pretty good newsboy, Mr. B. He sold out today's edition in two, three hours. Maybe we should keep him on."

The man whirled away from his desk and, barely giving me a glance, roared out, "Where's Henderson? I put him on that White Pass story this morning."

"Don't know, boss. Last time I saw him he was going toward the trailhead. How about sending the kid here to look for him?"

"I don't care who or what goes," the man said, looking past us to the doorway, where Persey stood watching. "As long as someone gets back in time to file a real story, and not some fairy tale about robbers on White Pass."

"Yes, sir," Shorty said, hustling me back into the pressroom and closing the door behind him. "Find Henderson and you'll have a place to sleep and maybe more."

"How will I know who to look for, Shorty?"

"He's a tall, skinny fellow wearing a brown suit and a green plaid cap. Sticks out like a sore thumb. I'd try the gambling houses if I was you."

I grabbed Persey and went out through the back. We walked the length of Broadway, up one side and down the other, and into side streets, poking our noses into nearly every establishment there was. I couldn't get over how much Skagway had grown in not even a year's time, and all the different kinds of folks bustling in and out and every which way. Finally, I spied a fellow in a green plaid cap watching a game of dice. I gave him Mr. Bigelow's message, which sent him off on a quick jog down the street, with me and Persey not far behind.

Bigelow tore into Henderson like he was going to skin him alive. I said to myself, *It would be good, maybe, to study this reporting business more before getting into it.*

Shorty told me that yelling was Bigelow's style, like it was in lots of newspaper offices. Best to stay out of his way when he was on a tear. I was about to say I have a sister like that, but caught it in time, having advertised myself as an orphan. The sudden thought of Ed made me feel kind of sad.

Shorty gave me some old blankets and said I could sleep under the press, like he'd done many a time. And so I did, with Persey at my side. It was pretty cool in the office, with no place to burn a fire, so she didn't mind so much being inside. In the morning I did whatever Shorty told me, and in the afternoon I walked all over town, hawking papers with Persey. I guess my old job with Miz Mulrooney had made me into a good worker and Shorty could see that, because he said I could stay on.

Just as soon as I was certain I had a job for keeps, I went back to our old cabin, keeping one eye out for Missus Kettleson and her dog, Rusty, so I wouldn't have to explain myself. I dug up Ma's tin box and took it back to the *Alaskan* office. I pried open the lid and had a quick look. Ma's copy of *Tales from the Arabian Nights* was lying on top, and I grabbed that, but left the rest for another time, when it might not remind me so sharp of what used to be. Shorty had cleared a shelf where I could stow my blankets during the day, and that's where I put the box, too.

It seemed like I was set up pretty good then. The only thing to worry about, Shorty said, was keeping out of Mr. Bigelow's way when he was on a rant. The person he ranted at most was Henderson.

"If I told you once, I told you a dozen times to lay off that stuff about the assay office, Jim. There's no story in it, no matter how folks try to make one, understand? No story at all!" he shouted once. That day it seemed like Henderson couldn't do anything right. Other times he and Mr. Bigelow would have their heads together, talking in low voices like they was in cahoots over something. Early on I came in with my broom in the middle of one of their talks.

"What are you doing here?" Mr. Bigelow roared. "I don't put up with people walking in here without a by-your-leave. Who are you, anyhow?"

"He's our newsboy, boss, and runs errands and sweeps up, too," Shorty said, limping in from the press-room. "You hired him last week."

"Well, we don't want him snooping around in here when we're talking business."

"No, sir," Shorty said. "I'll see that he don't."

After that I tried to keep out of Mr. Bigelow's view, which wasn't so easy because he was busy around town, just like me. I got my rounds set pretty fast. First I checked the wharf to see if any steamers had docked, bringing fresh customers. Then I'd go along to the hotels, starting with the Golden North, where folks stayed if they had any money. Not long after Mr. Bigelow bawled me out for snooping, I came into the lobby there and saw him glad-handing with some people, and he saw me, too. That made me kind of nervous, but I had a big stack of papers and the hotel was one of my best places, so I kept right on hawking the *Alaskan*.

That evening Mr. Bigelow came into the front office and sat down at his desk while I was sweeping. I backed off pretty fast. "I can finish this later, sir."

"No, no," he said, "keep on with your work." I could tell he was half watching me while he leafed through an account book. After a while he asked, "You peddle the *Alaskan* pretty much everywhere, don't you?"

"Yes, sir."

"And you hear people talking about one thing or another, probably."

"Well, yes, sir, they do talk."

He leaned back in his big desk chair and looked at me a while. "If you happen to hear something you think might make a news story, come and tell me. If it's interesting enough, we'll give you a little extra."

So there it was, what I wanted to do. Shorty had made fun of the idea, and here was Mr. Bigelow himself asking me to be a reporter. It was sort of like Miz Mulrooney all over again.

"Yes, sir," I said. "I had practice doing that and got pretty good at it."

"Of course, what you think is interesting I might not—so don't count on getting paid for just any piece of gossip."

"No, sir," I said. But I was already counting on making extra money to pay the gravestone maker, when I found one.

I commenced taking a little more time standing around after people had paid for their copy of the paper.

"Nice-looking dog you got there," someone might say, and I'd say, "Sure is, mister." Then, after he'd dug into his pocket for a dime and turned back to whoever he was talking with, I'd squat down and fiddle with the saddlebags I had made for Persey to carry papers in. Often enough folks would keep on talking, not seeming to notice I was there. I heard lots of stuff and carried most of it back to Mr. Bigelow without hardly adding any color at all.

"Folks are talking about how soon stampeders will be coming out with gold," I said one day, "being as breakup has already happened."

"When you hear something solid on that, let me know," he said. "And what's the talk about the Captain Smith's Widows and Orphans Fund?"

"They don't talk much about that in the Board of Trade," I said.

"Well, keep your ears open."

Sometimes he'd give me as much as a dollar for something he really liked, but none of it ever got into the paper as far as I could tell. Still, Mr. Bigelow seemed satisfied, and I was collecting a little stack of coins and beginning to think of myself as a newspaperman. Wouldn't my sister, Ed, be surprised if she could see me walking along with a half pencil stuck behind one ear? I didn't take notes much, of course, but it looked good.

One day I came across a man in a carpenter's apron, fixing some fancy edging for a new store going up. I sold him a paper and then asked if he knew anyone who made tombstones.

"Not yet. There's supposed to be someone coming in this summer. I hope you don't have need for a stone, young fella."

"It's for someone who died a while back," I said.

"Ah, well, most folks in Skagway make do with a wooden marker."

"I seen some of those. They don't look right, somehow."

"Depends who makes 'em," he said.

I agreed that was so and watched him a while longer.

"Might you carve me a wooden marker?"

"Sure, if I was to get paid—we could do business," he said.

So we agreed on it. I wrote out Ma's full name and when she was born, or close to, and the day and year she died. I asked about a rose, but he said that would cost considerable more than what we had agreed on.

Next time I came by, I gave him all I had and he said he'd do his best. He already had a nice cedar plank with Ma's name etched into it. "This'll last your lifetime, young fella," he said.

When it was finished, me and Persey carried it up to the burial ground, and I dug a place in the gravelly dirt as best as I could. I had to work a bit to keep the marker from toppling over or going lopsided, but at last I got it right enough.

"There, Ma," I said. "How do you like it? Don't you wish Edna Rose and Pa could see it, too?" I stood there admiring it a while before turning away.

On the way back to town I must've been lost in my thoughts, wondering about my folks, and I didn't notice I was going down our old road. Before I could get collected to run, there came Rusty, barking and leaping around, with his tail going to beat the band. And right on his heels Missus K. herself, apron on crooked and a dishpan in her hands. She stopped short, ready to fling dishwater to break up a dogfight. "Oh, my stars," she said. "Billy McGee, is that you?"

"Um, yes, ma'am."

"What are you doing here?"

Rusty galloped over to Persey, who bared her teeth, and I made like that took my attention while I was trying to think of a story. Maybe I could say I'd come up from Tacoma to fetch my pa home. A steamer from Seattle had docked a couple days before, making such a story seem possible, I thought.

It didn't seem to impress Missus K. much. Her eyes narrowed. "Your uncle sent a twelve-year-old boy up here on his own?"

"I'm going on fourteen, ma'am."

"Bring that big yellow dog on the steamer, did you?"

"Um, no, ma'am. She belongs to my friend Shorty down at the newspaper office."

"Newspaper office?"

"Yes, ma'am. I'm selling newspapers while I'm waiting for Pa. Would you like to have one? I'll get it for you free."

She waved that away. "I don't believe you're telling me the truth. I'll bet you run off from your uncle and stowed away."

That sounded good, so I tried to look sheepish like she'd hit on the truth.

"And what about that sister of yours? What's become of Edna Rose, the poor dear?"

"Huh?" I said. Nobody in his right mind would call my sister a poor dear. I patted Rusty to show Persey that he was all right, if overfriendly. "She's fine, ma'am. Not so stout as she used to be, but just as bossy."

"Of course, she's fallen off," Missus K. said. "A young girl losing her ma without warning like that. I knew it must've broke her spirit."

"No, ma'am," I says, hauling Persey away from Rusty. "Her spirit was never broke at all. Why, she bossed me all the way up the mountain and down the other side."

"Mountain?" Missus K. said.

I grabbed Persey's collar and, bending over, whispered, "Mush on," right in her ear. She took off and me with her, yelling over my shoulder, "So long, Missus Kettleson. Nice to see you again!" We ran all the way back to the *Alaskan,* Persey and me.

19

THE NEWS IN SKAGWAY

WELL, I'D FINALLY GIVEN Ma a proper marker, even if it wasn't stone, and wondered what I should do next. I couldn't see going all the way back to Grand Forks and Ed's bossing and not having a say in things—though I did wonder about the three of 'em often enough, especially now that Persey and me had settled into a routine at the *Alaskan*. I decided to stick with the newspaper work and see where that might take me.

I kept on hustling with the reporting business, picking up as much as I could, although it was getting harder to guess what would make Mr. Bigelow reach in his vest pocket for a coin. Trying to figure that was how I got into the telegraph office mystery, which seemed like something Mr. B. might really like. I knew about the telegraph office, of course, since it was in a tent cabin on State Street with a sign out front. Usually two, three men was waiting to send a message back home to

New York, or Seattle, or Chicago, saying they was all right or not all right and please send more money since they'd lost their grub stake. You knew that had most likely come about from them getting taken in by three-card monte or some other game of chance, but usually they didn't say so in the messages.

I was in the Board of Trade Saloon one afternoon, selling papers, and heard what seemed like the start of a pretty good fight having to do with the telegraph office. One fellow said he'd sent a telegram home and got an answer back the same day.

The fellow he was talking to said, "That's real interesting, seeing as there is no telegraph service between here and Seattle, let alone St. Louis."

The first man jumped up and swaggered a couple of steps toward the second one. "You calling me a liar? I tell you, I got an answer from my brother in St. Louie."

The second man went right on eating his fried eggs and sopping up the yolk with hunks of bread. "I never said you didn't get an answer. I just said it couldn't have come from St. Louis."

"You *are* calling me a liar, by gum!" yelled the first, and he doubled up his fists and danced around. The fellow eating eggs stood up, too, and wiped his hands on his shirt. It looked to be pretty lively there for a minute, until the barman stepped between them and said, "All right, boys, take it outside or stow it." They grumbled a bit, but then gave it over.

I was disappointed, since a fight about the telegraph office ought to make a really good story and I didn't have any other news that day. Still, it got me to wondering. Up to then I never thought about how telegrams got from here to there. They might have flown through the air for all I knew, but most likely, up here in Skagway, they got put on a steamer and taken south. If that was so, the fellow in the Board of Trade couldn't have got an answer for a couple weeks or more, like the other fellow said.

On the way back to the *Alaskan* office I went by way of State Street. I didn't see any wires coming out from the front of the telegraph office or the back, neither, when I snuck around there and looked. Maybe the wires were buried or ran along the ground somehow. But then I thought, to where? Down to the wharf, maybe? I was creeping along with Persey, looking for some evidence, when all of a sudden I was hauled up nearly out of my boots. A tough-looking man in a suit and a bowler had me firm in his grip.

"What are you doing here, buster?"

He shook me so hard, the coins in my pockets rattled. Persey began to growl low at the man, but I gave her a look and she stayed put.

"Looking for money I dropped," I said when I could get my breath.

"You dropped money here?"

"Somewhere around here."

He shook me again and said, "Go look for it somewhere else." But he didn't let go of my collar.

I was struggling to get away when the back door of the telegraph cabin opened and another man came out, an older man, also in a suit and a derby hat.

"Let the kid go, Sam. He hawks papers for Bigelow."

"Well, he ain't gonna sell any papers in our backyard."

"Maybe Bigelow is getting nosy. Someone will have to speak to him."

"Yeah," the first man said, giving me another shake before releasing me. "Scram, kid, and don't come back."

So I did scram, but figured I had some sort of story, bigger than the bits and pieces I'd been taking to Mr. Bigelow. If the man in the Board of Trade was right, how could you explain how the telegrams went anywhere? Wasn't that a front-page story? I might even get my name on it and some extra cash.

Mr. Bigelow did not agree. In fact, he hollered at me for being such a fool as to think something like a telegraph office would be news.

"If that's the kind of drivel you think we should print, I don't see you got a career in the news business."

"It's okay, Kid," Shorty said later. "There are some places you have to steer clear of, and the telegraph office is one of 'em. That and the assay office and Jeff Smith's Oyster Parlor. Should've told you that in the beginning."

"But why do I have to steer clear, Shorty?"

"Well, think about it, Kid."

Shorty went back to his typesetting, and I went back to listening to folks talk. I heard about a tent saloon up on White Pass where the railroad tracks were being laid. Rumors said it was run by one of Jeff Smith's boys and the railroad people didn't like it and was threatening to do something about it. I didn't set much store by a tale like that, but Mr. Bigelow was interested. In fact, he was almost always interested in anything about Jeff Smith.

Right then the *Alaskan* was filled with stories about the big Fourth of July celebration being planned for Skagway. In the spring of the year, around about the time we was digging on Skookum Hill, the U.S. had gone to war with Spain on account of a ship blowing up. Although most people didn't seem to know exactly why that led to war, they was eager to put on uniforms and march around with flags, and on the Fourth of July, especially. There was to be a big parade and Jeff Smith had been voted grand marshal, to lead it. There would be speeches and food and drink and fireworks for everyone. Mr. Bigelow had hardly anything else in the paper for a full week before, aside from ads, of course.

Still, even with all the celebrating, I got a feeling that something else was going on. Nothing I could tell exactly, but a feeling that life was getting meaner in the card rooms and saloons. The steerers, the ones who hustled people to go into certain gambling places, were bolder than before. You'd see a fellow standing outside a gambling place steering likely men inside for a game of chance. Course, they did that everywhere, but then I'd see the same fellow coming and going from Jeff Smith's Oyster Parlor, and that seemed to fit with what some folks were saying about how they was all in Smith's employ.

That week a prospector was robbed and killed on the White Pass Trail. Those same folks whispered that one of Smith's boys had done it. They said the gang was acting like they owned the trail and could do what they liked. Other people said there's no such thing as a Smith gang and anyone who held that opinion was a troublemaker. Mr. Smith, they said, was the town benefactor.

And he sure did look like one when he led the Fourth of July parade, mighty handsome in his black suit and riding a white horse. He was followed by the bunch of men he had recruited to fight the Spaniards in Cuba, only the secretary of war had wrote a letter saying they didn't need them. There was a brass band, firemen, and men from the Alaska Brotherhood, all marching in pretty good order with kids running alongside whooping and waving flags and now and again tossing firecrackers. After the parade the governor made a speech that lasted two hours. By the time it was over, everyone was pretty hungry and thirsty and dug into the free eats.

That day's entire edition of the *Alaskan,* with next to no news in it except about the Glorious Fourth, sold like hotcakes on a cold morning. We had to put out an extra edition, and I sold that one, too. Mr. Bigelow patted me on the head when I came around the speakers' stand hawking the paper and gave me an extra dollar.

"Well," I said to Persey, "things are going pretty good in this business."

Mr. Bigelow kept stories of the Glorious Fourth going for a day or two, but then interest in that began to peter out. Folks didn't want to read the governor's speech again, having had to sit through it live, and there didn't seem to be much else happening. So Persey and I went looking for something, snooping around the assay office and Smith's Oyster Parlor, where Shorty had told me to steer clear. Both places were closed in at the back by high board fences with no gates. When I shinnied up the fences and peered over the tops, there was nothing to see there, neither, only bare dirt yards and the back doors of the buildings.

A couple days after the Fourth, when I came through that same alley, I heard commotion and shouts seeming to come from the assay office yard. Then, right in front of me, like someone had said, "Open sesame," a door popped open in the board fence and a fellow tore through like the devil himself was at his heels. He ran right by me, but I don't believe he saw me at all, standing there with Persey, my mouth hung open. There was a terrible hullabaloo in the yard, sounds of doors slamming and people running around and shouting. One voice came up over all the rest. "My poke! He's run off with my poke!"

Other voices shouted, “Who? Where? Show me, I’ll get him!” but no one else came out of that door, and you couldn’t hardly tell it had ever been there.

Now, I thought, that story was surely better than a telegraph office where you couldn’t see the wires. I went over it in my mind and even put down a couple notes, to see could I make it better. Then I thought I’d try it out on Shorty, who was leaning back the way he did in his rolling chair, his hands playing over the typesetting keys but not making any type, just sitting there. I came around so I could see his face when I laid out my tale.

“I think I got a story—the beginnings, anyhow.”

“What’s that, Kid?”

“I happened to be going along Second Street, you know, back of the assay office, with that big old fence. All of a sudden a door you’d never know was there popped open and—”

I never got another word out because Shorty jumped up from his stool and whacked me. “Hey!” he yelled. “Get your hands off my Linotype.”

“What?” I said stupidly, and he whacked me again, so hard I almost fell over.

“I’ve told you before, Kid, don’t go messing with my machine,” Shorty said, grabbing me and swinging me around so I could see Mr. Bigelow standing in the doorway to the front office.

“Who told you to snoop around behind the assay office?” Mr. Bigelow asked, fixing me with a look would’ve fried ice. “Selling papers there, were you?”

"No, sir," I said, after Shorty gave me a shove. "I was just taking a shortcut back from the Golden North."

"Your job is to sell papers and not to snoop around back alleys. If you can't do that, I suggest you find another job."

"Yes, sir," I said. "Yes, sir." And I scuttled out, taking Persey with me.

Soon I heard a story, going like wildfire through the town, that I might've seen part of in that alley. Seems a young fellow by the name of Stewart had come down the White Pass Trail from Dawson, headed home to Canada with a poke full of gold dust. Folks told him to put it in a hotel safe until he shipped out, but he got to talking with a friend of Soapy's and ended up taking his gold into the assay office, where, he was told, he was bound to get a better price.

What happened then had happened lots of times before, according to Shorty, who whispered the whole thing to me when I dared to come back to the printing room.

"So this fellow hands over his poke to be assayed, and next thing he knows one of the friendly fellows that has been kidding around with him grabs it up like it was a game and dodges out the back door. Everyone else commences to yell and run around like they was helping. By the time the fellow—Stewart's his name, but ought to be "Sucker"—by the time he gets out the back door, he sees nothing but an empty yard and big board fence."

"His poke is clean gone?" I asked.

"What do you think? Of course it's gone. That's the way they operate."

"How come that ain't a story for the paper?"

"Sometimes, Kid, you act like you was hiding behind the kitchen door when they handed out the brains." He lowered his voice. "Mr. Bigelow is a friend of Soapy Smith. I mean a *good* friend, and that's what you need to keep in mind. Understand?"

"Not exactly," I said.

But right then Henderson came into the pressroom, and Shorty started talking about setting up some ads for the paper.

The rest of that day and into the night, the whole town buzzed with stories. Stewart went around telling anyone who would listen how he was robbed in the assay office of the poke he was taking home to his ma and pa. He went to the deputy sheriff, who told him the best thing to do was go back to the Klondike and get himself another poke. When they heard that, some folks said it was high time to take action.

"We can't have prospectors figuring they'll be robbed if they come through Skagway," one man said. "This town'll lose all the business."

"You bet," said another. "Time for the Vigilance Committee, ain't it?"

The next day when I went out with the paper, you could feel things was truly different, like a cloud was hanging over the town, despite the sun shining and a fair breeze blowing up the canal. The *Alaskan* seemed like something folks didn't want that day. They didn't want to read what was happening down in Cuba or what steamer was coming in. They was chewing their nails and muttering about what was going to happen in their own town.

Some merchants went to Mr. Smith's office in the Oyster Parlor and asked him to return Stewart's poke. The report was that Mr. Smith was outright insulted they should think he had that poor fool's gold dust. Then he said maybe somebody he knew had it and he might get it back. But as soon as that story went around, it got changed. Now, they said, Mr. Smith told the whole lot to go to Hades.

"We've had enough of him!" a man shouted, jumping up on the bar of the Nugget where I was peddling papers. "Get the Vigilance Committee together right now!"

I made a note to ask Shorty what was the Vigilance Committee next time we was alone. Early that evening, as Persey and me came back from my rounds, I could feel the change in the air for sure. The whole town was on edge, and even Persey was picking up on it and behaving kind of skittish. Something was about to happen. I just didn't know what.

20

THE BOSS OF SKAGWAY

BROADWAY WAS MOSTLY EMPTY, just a few people walking fast like they was trying to get somewhere. People were still in the places of business, all right—the saloons and eating houses—but they was all talking low and looking out, like they expected something. I came along slow with Persey, bringing back all the papers I had left over. The pressroom was empty—no Shorty—and the front office was empty, too. I sat down with my arm around Persey and watched the street.

In the middle of the evening Jeff Smith came out of his Oyster Parlor with a Winchester rifle slung over one shoulder and a pistol in his belt, looking neither to the right nor the left. He turned at the corner and headed for the wharf. I jumped up and trailed him at a safe distance. He hadn't got far down the road when Mr. Clancy, who sometimes worked in the Oyster Parlor, tried to stop him. Jeff Smith turned and lowered his

Winchester to the other fellow's chest. I couldn't hear what he said, but it must've been something fierce because Mr. Clancy threw up his hands and backed off, saying, "Okay, Boss, okay. It's your funeral."

Mr. Smith walked on, all alone, slow and deliberate like before. Other folks followed behind, keeping a good distance, like me and Persey. I looked around for Mr. Bigelow, or Henderson, or Shorty, but never saw hide nor hair of a one.

It was twilight then, like it would be until near midnight, and there was a kind of haze in the evening air and a stillness as the wind died away. Smith was too far ahead for me to see when the shots came, sharp and heart stopping. You could hear them for a mile up the canyon, folks said later. After that was dead silence. Then someone yelled, and a bunch of people came roaring down the wharf ramp toward us, running so hard the wood planks bounced. They was from the Vigilance Committee, people around us whispered.

"Two men down!" one shouted. "Send for the doctor!"

I sneaked in as close as I could get to the crowd of people who was gathered around two men lying stretched out. One of the men looked done for, and that was Jefferson Smith. The other one had his head raised up and was talking away, real excited.

"He got me, boys, but I got him first," he said.

"Who's that?" I whispered to a fellow next to me.

"Frank Reid," he said. "He was standing guard for

the Vigilance Committee when Soapy Smith come with his Winchester to rush the meeting."

"And did they shoot each other just like that?"

"Looks that way, don't it?"

Frank Reid was lifted up by four or five committee men and carried off the wharf toward the doctor's place. A big crowd had gathered by then and he waved as he went by, saying, "I got him, boys. He got me, too, but I got him first."

There was lots of action on the street, people running around, skittering this way and that, like they didn't know what they was doing or the world was coming to an end.

After I saw Mr. Reid carried into Dr. Whiting's place, I went back to the *Alaskan* office, ready to write up my story or tell it, anyhow. The front door was closed and locked. I could hear noise inside, but no one answered my banging. I went around back and found that door hanging wide open. Before I reached it, out came Henderson, carrying a sizable carpetbag.

"Jim," I said, "you missed the biggest story of the year!" He never answered a word, but staggered across the yard, heaved his bag over the fence, and shinnied over after it.

"Where're you going?" I yelled, but never got an answer to that, neither. No one was in the pressroom, but there was noise in the front. Turned out to be Mr. Bigelow, stuffing papers into the potbellied stove that was fired up and blazing away.

"I got a big story for you, sir. There's been a shootout, and Mr. Smith is stone dead and Frank Reid bad wounded and taken up to Doc—"

He always did scare me, Mr. Bigelow, so when he swung his arm like he was going to whack me, I moved quick out of the way. He didn't come any further, just turned back to putting papers in the fire. When he was done with that, he stuffed some things in a carpetbag even bigger than Henderson's and went right through the pressroom and out the back door. Being too stout to shinny over the fence, he pried off three, four boards with a claw hammer, then squeezed himself and his bag through the hole. I followed him a while, until I lost him among the shacks on that side of town.

So there was only me and Persey left. We bedded down under the press as usual, but couldn't hardly sleep for the sounds of people running around in the street and shouting.

Next morning Shorty came in. The front office was a mess, papers still smoldering in the wood stove, desk drawers hanging open, shelves half cleared, and the till empty. He checked that first thing while I was telling what I knew, in case he hadn't heard.

"So since Mr. Bigelow and Henderson run off, I guess you and me will have to put out the paper. We could do a single sheet, couldn't we? With a couple of sketches? I'll find out how Frank Reid is coming along and we'll put that in. What do you think, Shorty?"

He glanced at me in the middle of hauling out stuff

from shelves in the pressroom. "Kid, didn't I tell you Bigelow was in cahoots with Soapy Smith?"

"We can put that in, too."

He was packing tools and other stuff in a grip and barely stopped to speak. "We ain't gonna put anything in any paper, because there ain't gonna be any paper."

"But, Shorty . . ."

I followed him from one room to the other while he rummaged around looking for what, I didn't know—tools, mostly. "I brought these," he muttered, "and by gum, I'm gonna take 'em back."

When his grip was stuffed full, he strapped it up and turned to me. "If you take my advice, Kid, you'll clear out, just like I'm doing, before the vigilantes take a notion we was in cahoots with the Smith gang, too, and haul us off to jail like they're doing all them others."

"But, Shorty," I said, "that don't make sense. The whole town turned out to cheer Jeff Smith not four days back. Is everyone gonna be nabbed?"

"Some will," he said, "and I ain't taking any chances. They got Reverend Bower already and Old Man Tripp, too, while he was sitting down to dinner at the Pancake Palace, saying he'd rather hang on a full stomach."

"That'd be really good for the story. We could make money on a paper, you and me. I'll do the reporting and you can set the type."

I stopped then because he was looking at me so grim, his chipmunk cheeks didn't even wobble. "You are determined to play dumb, ain't you, Kid? Listen, now, and I'll say it slow. Bigelow was being paid by Smith's men to print what Soapy wanted and leave out what he didn't want, and a lot of folks know that. Anybody connected with the paper is gonna be looked on unfavorable."

"But, Shorty, you and me didn't have anything to do with that, did we? Why would the vigilantes be after us?"

"Who knows?" he said. "When folks get worked up, you can't tell what they'll do. If Reid don't make it, they'll be talking about hanging somebody, is my guess. Me, I'm headed south on the first boat I can find." He slung the heavy grip clanking with tools over his shoulder.

"Kid," he said, turning at the back door, "I'd like to help you, I really would, but I got family back in Frisco to worry about. You lay low a couple of days and you'll be all right, I expect. You know that Missus Kettleson that advertises her pies in the paper? She asked after you the other day and seemed friendly. My advice—stay with her until folks cool off. So long, Kid." With that he was out the door and gone, and with him my new life as a newspaper reporter.

I felt pretty low then. Persey poked her nose into my hand like she understood what a pickle we was in. We had a place to sleep probably, but then what? Would I have to go to Missus K. and be jawed at, and maybe get turned in as a runaway?

I hung around the newspaper office all the rest of that day and into the next, peering out now and again. Men I recognized as part of the Vigilance Committee still roamed the streets, hunting fugitives. I sneaked over to what was left of the Oyster Parlor in the evening. It had been rummaged through pretty bad, but still I found some tinned crackers and took 'em for Persey and me. Then I went back to the pressroom and began sorting through my own stuff, deciding what I would take. Not much: a couple dime novels I had picked up, the *Arabian Nights* book, some castoff clothes folks had given me, a notebook for stories that hadn't come to anything, and Ma's tin box that I had looked in once and set aside. I took out to the back step, pried it open, and spilled everything out.

Here was the stuff we had put away, my tin soldiers and marbles that I didn't care for no more and my sister's autograph album from when she was in school in Tacoma. Most of the rest was Ma's treasures: A photograph of her and Pa when they married, her standing stiff and tall, all buttoned into a dark dress with a high white collar, and Pa with a high collar, too, sitting beside her, just as stiff. I had seen the picture before, but now it struck me how strange it was that my folks had been young once. There was some silver buttons cut off that dress she was married in, a packet of silk and velvet scraps she must've been saving for a crazy quilt, a book of poems she used to recite out loud, and, in the very bottom of the box, a notebook full of recipes. I put the box down and went through the notebook page by page, looking for a message among the rules for making beaten biscuits, rabbit stew, and applesauce cake, like the one Edna Rose threw into the chicken coop after saying I had ruined it.

"See, Ma," I said, "that's Edna Rose all over, still cutting off her nose, like you used to say."

It seemed an answer came to me: *No, that ain't exactly Edna Rose, leastways last time you saw her.*

"Ha," I said. "Then she's just hiding it." And I went on leafing through the notebook. Some places there was dates telling when Ma had got the recipe and the name of who she got it from. Sometimes there was a couple words about how something turned out. "Gip says don't try this again" was one, and another was "Billy likes these flapjacks with blueberries." I traced over the words several times with my finger, until they blurred.

Then I put everything back in the box and got up to finish my packing, but it seemed like something held me there with that box in my hands. I looked around for what it was. Then it came to me, like I'd been struck.

"Ma," I said, "I left our folks without saying goodbye, just like you done, Ma. Just like you done." When I heard myself say that, I began to bawl like the crybaby Ed had named me, and then I bawled some more, glad she wasn't there to see it. After a long time I brushed a sleeve across my eyes and went inside.

21

MY SISTER, ED, AGAIN

EARLY THE NEXT MORNING I rolled my stuff into a bundle I could carry. “We’re going up to Barker’s place,” I said to Persey. “We can sleep in the barn and maybe get work on his pack train. If that don’t work out, I’ll have to try Missus K. I ain’t beat yet, Persey, and you ain’t, neither.”

I closed the pressroom door and set off. Since I was still trying to keep out of sight, even that early, I circled around eastward behind Mrs. Pullen’s hotel and went up toward the burial ground, thinking to stop and tell Ma all that had happened. I was going over the story in my mind—to add a little color, like Miz Mulrooney would say, although it didn’t need much—when I heard my name spoke out. There, coming down from the burial ground, was a person wearing boots and a calico dress and a big brimmed hat.

“Billy, is that you?” the person said, taking off the

hat so her brown curls shone in the early light. When I saw who it was, I nearly fell over. I couldn't believe it. My sister, Ed.

"What are you doing here?" I asked when I got my senses back.

"Looking for you," she said.

"Up in the graveyard? Well, I ain't buried, yet."

She sucked in her breath and said, "Oh, Billy, what made you run off that way and leave us not knowing whether you were alive or dead?"

"If you're looking for the nuggets I took, it's too late. I spent 'em all buying Persey back, like Pa promised he would and didn't."

She nodded, and her hair that had grown out curly wriggled and bounced. It was the liveliest thing about her, as the rest looked kind of puny. "If you'd asked him, he would've, Billy, especially if he knew you was planning to run off."

"Huh," I said, somehow doubting that but not knowing what else to say.

"We took the first boat after breakup to come look for you and have been looking all the way from Dawson."

"We?"

"Jack and me. Pa wanted to come but his feet got so bad, he didn't think he could. He wouldn't let me go alone, so Jack came along, and we left Pa to guard the claim."

"That so?" Since I had told Pa about Ed and Jack before I run off, I guessed that meant he'd given them his blessing. For some reason the idea of them maybe getting hitched at some point didn't bother me near so much as it would have just a few months ago.

"At first we thought maybe you had drowned in the breakup and we were almost destroyed with sorrow. Then that man, that Mr. Garr, came back and said you were alive last time he saw you, going south on the trail where folks are robbed and killed all the time." She came down the little slope to where I was standing. "Oh, Billy," she said, holding out her hands, "we're looking for you to bring you home."

"Grand Forks ain't home."

"It's where your folks are and where you're wanted," she said.

I couldn't answer that, so I shifted from one foot to the other, then put my bundle down and patted Persey. I thought again about how Pa had taken her from me. But then I thought, too, about all the trouble Ed and me went through after Ma died to find him, just so I could turn around and run off from him. "I been working in the newspaper business here, studying to be a reporter. I don't know as I could leave."

"There's going to be a newspaper in Dawson," Ed said. "I'll bet you could study reporting there, too."

"Well, I don't know. Maybe I'll think about it."

"Good," she said, with a little bit of the old Ed spirit. "That's a nice marker put up for Ma."

"I guess it'll do until I get enough money for a stone."

"Maybe Jack could carve a rose on it like you wanted."

"Oh, Jack," I said. "He didn't know Ma."

"He says I told him so much he feels like he did."

You can't answer something dumb like that, so I said, "He was my friend before he was yours."

"I know that, Billy."

"And he wouldn't have thought to look for a bench claim without what I told about Axel."

"I know that, too."

It looked like she wasn't going to give me any back talk, so I asked, "Where is he, anyhow?"

"That's one of my troubles, Billy. First was losing you, and now it's losing Jack."

"Did he run off on you, too?"

"No," she said, "he was nabbed."

"Nabbed?"

"We were coming down the White Pass Trail and lost one another when we came up against some sort of posse. I think maybe Jack got caught in a roundup by mistake."

"Could be," I said, thinking it over. "The vigilantes was out looking for men in the Smith gang. Jack might have fit that description."

"Do you think so?"

"Likely," I said, hauling up my bundle again. "I know this town pretty good, and I can find him if he's here. I'll tell you the whole shebang that led up to this. It's a real good story, Ed."

While we walked back toward town, I told my sister about the man called the Boss of Skagway and his con men, and how after he got gunned down, a posse of vigilantes went looking for everyone that had been in his employ. "I knew some of 'em firsthand," I said, "and was even working for one, but didn't really know that until a few days back. Should've, though."

"Oh, my," she said, looking at me kind of respectful.

It didn't take me long to find out that Jack was in the big log building they called the City Hall, which was being used as a jail for all the folks the vigilantes had caught. The guard said they snagged everyone that answered to a certain description, and Jack Purdy, carrying a poke full of nuggets and being pretty grubby and shifty looking, fit right in.

"But him and me just came down from the Klondike with those nuggets," my sister said. "We were still on the trail."

The guard shrugged. "You can tell that to the judge." Then he said everyone had to wait for the U.S. commissioner, Judge Sehlbrede, to decide what to do with the prisoners.

Ed heated up, more like her old self. "Shifty looking and lacking a bath?" she said. "Is that all it takes to jail a man in this town?"

"Now, whoa," said the guard. "Ma'am, are you talking against law and order?"

I had to haul her away before she got thrown in jail, too.

The hearing took place that same morning, and me and Ed was among the first to crowd into the room. Looked like the whole town was there, most of them wanting to see justice done to thieves and sharpers who was giving Skagway such a bad name.

A big desk stood on a platform at one end of the room, with an American flag on each side. The portly man who came in and sat down at the desk looked not so different from Reverend Bower or Mr. Bigelow, but now they was on the opposite side and likely to have to beg mercy from him. The prisoners were brought in one or two at a time for the judge to hear their story and for anyone to give evidence. Mostly it was to agree to whatever the accusation was.

I knew a good many of the prisoners from my days of going in and out of saloons and gaming parlors. The man from the telegraph office was hauled in, sweating and mumbling to himself.

"Ask him how come he charged five dollars for every message going out, when there weren't no place for 'em to go!" someone shouted.

"He wrote 'em himself and charged five dollars for the answer!" another person yelled, and the telegraph man, who used to wear a derby hat and smoke big cigars, looked around like he feared a lynch mob would be forming up. But Judge Sehlbrede banged for order and said he was the only one could tell people when to talk and when not. After he questioned the man about the telegraph service, he said he took a dim view of bunco artists.

"You'll be sent to the grand jury at Sitka. You can tell them your story. Next."

That same judgment took care of Reverend Bower and Old Man Tripp, the one who declared if he was going to be hanged, he would be hanged on a full stomach, by gum. Looked like there wasn't going to be any hanging of anyone. Some were hustled off to Sitka, and another bunch was to be sent down to Seattle and maybe be greeted with outstanding warrants. Mr. Bigelow, looking shrunken, with his eyes darting around every which way, was one of those. Looked like he hadn't gotten away quick enough and got nabbed. He said he was only reporting the news, but other people testified they had heard him and Smith's men talking about what should be in the *Alaskan* and that he never printed anything that Jeff Smith didn't like.

Shorty and Henderson must've got on a boat, because they didn't seem to be among the ones that had been nabbed by the vigilantes. *Where is Jack?* I was beginning to wonder. But after Mr. Bigelow was led off, three fellas were brought out and one was Jack Purdy.

"Does anyone wish to bring evidence for or against these persons?" Judge Sehlbrede wanted to know. There was a chorus against them and only one in favor, and that was me.

"Sir!" I hollered after my sister gave me a poke. "Permission to speak."

The judge leaned over his desk and peered down at me. "State your name and business, young man."

"William McGee, sir, and I know that one with pink hair. His name is Jack Purdy and he ain't any part of Smith's gang—I'll vouch for that, sir."

"How do you know this person?"

"He's partners with my pa and my sister and me on the Bonanza," I said. "We been up there all year prospecting and hit pay dirt this spring. That's how come he had nuggets with him. That Stewart fellow that got robbed, he had gold dust, not nuggets. Can't be the same poke, Your Honor."

"I don't need you to be telling me what evidence we're looking for, young fellow," the judge said, frowning.

Someone yelled, "Don't believe that kid! He was on the street every single day peddling Bigelow's rag and probably spying for him, too."

"Yeah," said someone else. "I saw him hanging around Smith's establishments several times."

"Is this true?" the judge asked, glaring down at me.

I took a breath. People was staring now, and not with friendly looks, neither. Ed clutched my arm, like she feared I'd be nabbed, too.

"I was snooping for my own information," I said, "not for Mr. Bigelow." That was close to the truth, if not right on it. "In fact, I was on the trail of figuring out the game at the telegraph office when the whole thing blew up."

"Hmm," said the judge.

"I only been working at the *Alaskan* a little while, anyway. How could I know Mr. Bigelow was in cahoots, sir?"

"I'll ask the questions," the judge said. "Anyone here able to vouch for this youth?"

My sister said she could, but otherwise the room was silent. One of the deputies started toward me, like he was going to drag me off. I jumped out of my seat and onto the platform and looked all through the crowd. With Shorty gone, there was only one other person in town who knew me apart from being Bigelow's paperboy.

"Judge," I said, "you can't be making decisions without you have all the facts."

"Young fellow, you tell me once more what I can or can't do and I'll have you jailed for contempt."

"Beg pardon," I said, "but please send someone to get Missus Kettleson. You know, the pie lady. She lives right up the road and has been here from the beginning and knows me and my sister and my ma, Rose Ellen McGee, who's buried up yonder."

The crowd murmured and shifted around, and finally a fellow went out the door, hollering for Missus Kettleson.

"I'll give you five minutes," the judge said. He asked for someone to bring him a cup of coffee while we waited. Pretty soon in she came, Missus K., apron askew like usual and no time to tie her bonnet strings.

“Why, Billy McGee,” she called out when she spied me. “What are you doing here?”

“You know this young man?” the judge asked.

“Surely I do, and his pa and sister, and his ma that’s passed on.”

“Would you say he might be a member of the Smith gang?”

“Of course not. I don’t believe he’d have the gumption. Well, he might have gumption, all right, because he came back to Skagway on his own, ain’t that right, Billy?”

“Yes, ma’am,” I said.

“But he isn’t one bit crooked,” she added. “I’ll vouch for that.” Then she launched into a tale of how our pa went off on the gold rush trail leaving us with our ma who took sick and died before a body could turn around and how me and Edna Rose took care of her so devoted—

“That will do, ma’am,” Judge Sehlbrede cut in. “We don’t have time for more history. Young man, you are dismissed. I hope you’ve learned a good lesson.” He didn’t say about what, and I didn’t ask, but went back to sit with Ed and Missus. K., who squeezed herself in beside us.

After a few more questions and whispering with one of his deputies, Judge Sehlbrede banged his gavel and declared that Jack Purdy was free to go, along with three or four others that had got swept up on the White Pass Trail and for which there was no evidence connecting them with the Smith gang. Nobody apologized, and some folks muttered that justice wasn't being done, but me and Ed held up our heads as we marched out. It took a little while for Jack to get his poke back, but pretty soon there he was, too.

Next thing we was all in the roadway, looking at one another—Missus K., Jack Purdy, my sister, and me.

Jack put out his hand. "Much obliged, Billy," he said. "This is the second time you saved me."

"That's all right," I said. "Probably you would've got off anyhow."

"Sooner is better than later," he said, and I had to agree, as he looked a good deal worse for the wear.

"We appreciate your assistance, Missus Kettleson," my sister said.

"Think nothing of it, my dear. It was my pure pleasure. Now, if you don't mind my saying so, you all look puny. I expect you haven't had your breakfast."

"That's true," my sister said.

"Come along to my place for blueberry biscuits with ham. We can catch up on our news and find out how it is that Billy come to be in Skagway with that big yellow dog."

I had forgot Persey and ran to where I had tied her. Then Jack and Missus K. started off, gabbing with one another about whether Jack's people came from the same old country as Missus K., while Ed hung back waiting for me.

Me and her walked up the road toward where our old cabin was and the place where we had buried Ma's things.

"I dug up the box," I said. "It's in my bundle right now."

"That's good, Billy. I worried about it the whole year."

"Did you?" I asked. "You never peeped a word."

"People don't always say everything they're thinking." After a while she added, "Should we leave the grave marker as it is or get one made of stone?"

"I guess it depends on if I stay here or go back on the gold rush trail with you and Jack."

She stopped dead in the road and turned to look at me. "Why did you run off?"

I remembered most of my reasons, but I couldn't trot 'em out. "I don't know. I wanted to do something on my own, I guess."

"It ain't family without you."

"You might've said that earlier."

"How was I to know you had it in mind to run off?"

I mulled that over for a time. "Well," I said finally, "none of you ever asked."

I put my arm around her shoulders, noting that either I had grown or she had shrunk, because I was taller than her now. We walked on for a time without speaking, then I stopped and said, "There's something I been meaning to ask. You remember that last day when Ma was so sick? Did you ever figure out what she was trying to tell us?"

"No, Billy. I wouldn't let myself think about it."

"Well, I did," I said, "and it has finally come to me."

"What?" she asked, kind of muffled.

"She wanted to say goodbye."

"Oh," my sister said. "Oh, Billy." She bowed her head. I kept my arm around her and patted her shoulder as best I could.

After a while we walked on that way, me and my sister, Ed, headed toward our breakfast and the gold rush trail once more.